SCENE

THROUGH A WINDOW

SCENE THROUGH A WINDOW

A Historical Romance

BY

MARCY HEIDISH

Dolan & Associates, Publisher

SCENE THROUGH A WINDOW

Copyright © 2014 by Marcy Heidish

**LIBRARY OF CONGRESS CATALOGING-IN-
PUBLICATION DATA**
Heidish, Marcy.
Library of Congress Control Number: 2014937739
ISBN: 978-0-9831164-7-9

Cover art: central image of 13th century stained glass window
called *Notre-Dame de la Belle Verriere* in Notre-Dame de
Chartres Cathedral depicting the Marriage at Cana, Author
Vassal released this work worldwide into the public domain.

Chartres Cathedral [p. 236 herein]: High Gothic view from
southeast; May 24, 2010; a file from the Wikimedia Commons,
licensed under the Creative Commons Attribution-Share
Alike 3.0 Unported license; Author: Olvr.

Dolan & Associates, Publisher
Printed in the United States of America
....
First edition

For
the nameless glass-makers, sculptors and
builders of Chartres Cathedral

and

in memory of
U.S. Colonel Welborn Barton Griffith, Jr.

The light shines in the darkness,
and the darkness has not overcome it.
— The Gospel of John, 1:15 ESV

I never spoke with God,
Nor visited in heaven,
Yet certain am I of the spot
As if the chart were given.
— Emily Dickinson

CHARTRES, FRANCE

1196

I wrote what I remember and my memory is long. It reaches back into my childhood at the stone hem of a queenly presence: The Cathedral of Our Lady of Chartres. Famed in Europe as a pilgrimage shrine, it stood as a majestic mother: prized, proud and, we believed, protected from disaster.

But what on earth remains so protected?

In a single night, wind-whipped flames ravaged most of our Cathedral and parts of our town, small but ancient, winding up a hill amid the cornfields of La Beauce. The fire burst upon us on a Friday, I remember, hot and clear, the tenth of June in the year of Our Lord, 1194.

The loss was inexpressible.

The cause was unidentified.

The outcome was miraculous.

Three days after this fire, priests emerged from the cathedral's crypt with Chartres' precious relic, still intact: a sign, a blessing, and an inspiration to rebuild what was lost.

Immediately, a daring new cathedral was envisioned; one to surpass any that had gone before. This mighty work is already well begun and I am pleased to see it as I return to Chartres.

Now, as I edge along the building site, I am still recognized by the townsfolk here. They see my unruly red hair, ever escaping its confines, my tall form and fair skin. I'm told I have a fragile look; few people note my strength and my capable hands.

No longer the girl they may remember, I am still a young woman, tried by life and certainly by fire, who stands back and gazes about with uncommon intensity. But why?

Here I see what is *not* visible. I note what wavered on this ground two years ago: an imagined structure, dreamed and drawn and driven into its beginnings. The past opens wider as I watch; it reveals the hidden history behind the raising of a great cathedral.

With all its twists and tangles, here lies an unknown story. I cannot sing of it in a ballad and I cannot set it into verse. I am no saint, God knows, nor royalty, nor scholar. Even so, I had an unseen part in this astonishing renewal.

~~~

About myself there is little to say.

My father was the only man to die during childbirth—mine. Shouting for the midwife, he fell headfirst out an upstairs window; my mother lost a husband as she gained a child. He was a glass-painter who worked with his wife, far more gifted than he. Perhaps you know of her, Sabina Fay. Her brush strokes adorn the windows of Counts and Cardinals.

Like many widows, my mother carried on her husband's trade. She took me with her as she worked, from princely homes to parish churches: wherever art was needed for stained glass windows. I delighted in my apprenticeship to her; she also taught me how to read and write, and I postponed marriage for our work.

Why, then, did she wed that red-faced rogue Henri Dufort? Granted, he was the most prosperous baker in town, but Sabina Fay had her own inheritance. I think the reason was simple: indiscretion. Only seven months after she wed, it was my mother who died in childbirth. I had little time to grieve.

Now, as Dufort's stepdaughter, I had to turn my hand from paint to pastry. I sculpted crème-filled "castles," sweet-meats shaped as "swans," and cakes-as-crowns, all tinted with my signature glazes. The rough-tongued baker found me "too outspoken for a female" but he found me useful to filling his coffers.

Whenever a ball or a banquet was planned, their hosts ordered my tarts and custom-made centerpieces. I was called "the baker's daughter," more often than I was called by name: Cecile Dufort, *pâtissière par excellence.* Not exactly my answer to prayer but how often in life do such answers come?

In truth, I knew little of life then, and even less of men. I did not know how common routine could change in moments, how love could upend everything, nor did I know anything of real love itself, beyond the lore of troubadours: wild love, untamed, unlimited.

For now, I must make do and be grateful. I had moved into an ample house with absent half-brothers, two glass windows, and a pear tree in the garden. No one was forcing me to marry; my step-father wanted me to make pastry, not babies. Not *now*, not *yet*, not *here*, he shouted with malice in his eyes.

What *did* I know in those simpler days? Little, really, except the workings of my trade, the cycling of the seasons, the cruelties and beauty of this life, the need for women's modesty and, of course, God's presence everywhere.

Bread, too, was everywhere in this small town, as it is now. The smells of yeast and dough hung over us like voices in the air. And above them, the presence of our great cathedral, rising like some magical horned creature, speaking to us through its bells. Bread and bells and bills: these were the constants of my life.

What else can I remember of that time?

The scent of mist and mint and marigolds floating near our river. Winter evenings when the air went purple. Summer sun shattering like glass in a rain barrel. Birds arrowing through the narrow streets and berries bright as embers. Simple things, taken for granted—before the disaster that divided our lives.

We always called it the Great Fire:

I cannot forget the sight of blazing houses and the old cathedral flaring like a torch against the night sky. Flames spread like fever through leaning, wooden dwellings, turning some to ash but sparing others, like our own. People ran, children fell, men and women emptied bucket after bucket. I saw it all in a red and hellish glow.

A few moments earlier, this had been an ordinary Friday night. Fairly ordinary, I should say. It was one year after the town was walled. It was the eve of a saint's feast day. St. Barnabas, in fact. It was also the eve of my eighteenth birthday—and the eve of true womanhood for me, I see as I look back.

On the cusp of this new season in my life, a new season began for Chartres. Here designers must create a sanctuary where heaven and earth would flow together and reflect God's gaze in stone and in stained glass. The cathedral must offer a glimpse of the Heavenly Jerusalem—right here.

Such a place must light the wheeling years, the turning centuries, the coming generations, the trudging pilgrims yet unborn. A daunting task indeed, even for the most expert, the most exceptional, the most experienced of men.

Even so, ambitious artists of every age were gathering in Chartres: men ready to compete for coveted commissions. The Master of Works was all but chosen, as was the Master Mason who would oversee a vast amount of statuary and sculpture.

Yet to be selected was the Master Glazier, or glass-maker, or so we heard. I painted with my own homemade colors on the wall of our loft and wished I could join those competitors for the honor of designing the new stained glass windows.

The names of most contenders were "officially" unknown, but several men, we knew, would soon present samples of their work. Among the judges: our powerful Bishop, his assistant, members of the Cathedral Chapter, and the Cathedral School.

Unofficially, certain nobles and influential donors would have their say. I had not heard of any artists among the judges; this lack seemed odd to me. But who was I to say? The judges' standards would be high. Marvels were demanded.

~~~

And now these marvels are well underway. Our new cathedral will be built and carved and windowed in a single generation: my own. Such a feat is extraordinary even in these modern times, as we near the momentous year of 1200.

Amazing as it sounds, I am a fragment of such marvels. I hold dear those early days of plans and preparations—and the secret of our new and dazzling blue, seen in samples, viewed by all. This color may be imitated but never equaled. I know. I happened to be present at the time of its creation.

It seems right for wonders to appear at Chartres, known to be the font of many miracles. I love this terraced town climbing the hill toward the cathedral. A day's ride from Paris, this is a place of no minor significance, despite its small size.

We have a noted Cathedral School, a renowned scholastic center, and a thriving marketplace for a wide variety of goods. Theologians, scholars and merchants gather here. Not to mention floods of pilgrims who arrive each year to venerate our sacred relic. Even as children we were proud of Chartres.

Years of peace and plenty formed the background of my childhood. I grew into girlhood and early womanhood, treasuring my independence, such as it was, as well as my home. Never did I see myself living anywhere but here.

But how much of the future can we see?

My life was abruptly reshaped again, much to my shock and sorrow. Against my will, I had to leave my birthplace and my home. Even in Paris, where I learned much, I always thought myself an exile. There I grew familiar with quills and silks, words and worldly things, but Chartres remained the core of me.

At last, I have been able to come back. Moments ago, I arrived in the old town and went directly to the new cathedral's building site. There I stand now, savoring the feel of it, the hum of it, the spill of my remembrances. I want to see what was here for me once and what may yet be here for me.

During these last painful years, I have written out a story, perhaps not quite finished. You will never find it in any chronicle or history or record. This is my unofficial and intimate account of events "behind the screens," as it is said.

If anyone should read my words and doubt them, I challenge him to open his mind. Think thus: "Here is a story behind a story—and here is how it might have gone." In any case, this account has become my calling and, perhaps, my penance as well.

I still think of it that way:

My penance.

As a girl I harbored a secret so unspeakable I could not bring it to confession. Right or wrong, I bore the guilt of burning down the most honored and hallowed place any of us knew: the old cathedral, Our Lady of Chartres.

■

CHARTRES, FRANCE
1194

To burn down the Queen of Heaven's earthly palace is enough to scald and scar the soul.

You cannot apologize.

You cannot make excuses.

You cannot restore the loss.

In fact, you cannot speak of it or sleep on it or keep it from your thoughts. Destroying a cathedral is a strange kind of slaughter. It would shake the strong, the wise, the venerable, and I was none of these when the fire began.

You must have patience with me. I was only young and blamed myself for what I thought I'd done. Let me be clear on one point, however. This is not an arsonist's confession; I did not set a fire by intention or design. At the time, that fact did not seem to matter much to me. The unspeakable had happened, perhaps by my hand—that was all I knew and that was my torment.

Some said a lightning bolt struck the Cathedral's North Tower, thus starting the fire. Only an act of God could take down such a church, the old ones believed. The skies were clear that night, others argued, though lightning can dart from nearby storms, as yet out of sight.

Even so, everyone agreed the North Tower stood firm and seemed unscathed. I walked away from those airing their notions about the Great Fire. My secret whereabouts as it commenced was enough to convince me of my guilt.

Now, by night, I courted peril and penance as I rambled the cathedral's ruins, once they had cooled. This I did without a light, under a waning moon, soon after the Great Fire.

Both of the cathedral's towers had survived, alongside the West Wall, often called the Royal Portal. Its many statues and sculptures remained intact, as did its glass and the crypt below.

And that was all. The ruins looked the way I pictured a lunar landscape: a mess of melted lead and crumbled stone and blackened beams skewed at crazy angles, though the strong foundation stood firm.

Now the cathedral brought to mind a fractured and desecrated skeleton. It certainly put me in mind of death, though there were no tombs beneath this church. And was it death I wooed, those hours when I stumbled through the rubble?

Was I hoping some loose beam would fall and mete out my the punishment I felt I deserved?

Indeed I was.

At the time, this was my wish: A fatal "accident" would be a fitting end to me and my inner turmoil. Ordinarily, I was not a morbid girl, given to unwholesome brooding. But this was no ordinary time. This was no ordinary event. This was the cathedral. I could not put the fire from my thoughts. Every night, it burned its way into my sleep and lit my dreams:

That warm evening, that shifting dry wind. The couples kissing in the hedgerows—dry hedgerows, wilting from two weeks of rainless days.

I see myself going to the cathedral where I always lit tapers on my birthday eve. I see the old hump-backed sexton on his knees as if in prayer, but his wizened face sags in sleep; his white-thatched head bobs above his narrow shoulders.

Now I see the nave opening ahead: a dark lake-like space, and the bank of votive candles to the left, in the north transept, beneath a clutch of hanging banners: yellow, green, blue, red.

As if from above, I watch my hand holding a lit taper, reaching over other tapers to place mine nearest to the statue of Our Lady. I do not notice how my sleeve dips and skims the dancing flames.

Eyes closed, I am offering prayers of praise and petitions, so many petitions, when I feel the heat around my wrist. My eyes open on my sleeve, now curling with fire.

I watch the cloth fall, blazing, into the bank of lighted tapers. Tearing off my tunic, I try to smother the flames. My eyes dart about for sand buckets; they are close but too heavy for me to lift.

Shouting, gasping, I shake the sexton awake and push him toward the shrine and sand. He doesn't see me just behind him—only the flames. And then I'm running out the nearest door, seeking help I cannot find nearby...

No one knew that I had been in the cathedral, I felt sure. No one saw me moving toward it; of this I made certain. And afterwards, no one knew my guilt, twisting like a snake within me.

Would the secret show in my pale face, blue eyes and full but trembling lips? Perhaps in the tendrils of my wild red hair, slightly singed across the forehead? But there were others who staggered, singed and scorched, through our town in the fire's aftermath. Unnoticed, I passed among them.

The loss of the cathedral was a lasting shock— not only to me but to everyone in Chartres, even as new plans and preparations were begun. Earlier cathedrals had been built and burned here, I knew. Even so, I could not remember them nor could I recall the firestorms that had carried them away.

Fire: it was always on our minds. There were often small ones in the town; our houses, clustered close together, passed flames along like plague. Every household, every shop kept at least one tub of sand beside the kitchen fire and buckets by all doors.

We watched and sniffed for smoke with constant care. This was true in the new towns springing up in meadows everywhere, it seemed: Hamlets rising and, too often, burning down.

These distant fires were familiar sights to us— familiar as the farmers in the fields and the troubadours at fairs. I listened to their tales of tournaments and knights and castles but these were not part of my world.

My world was the ancient town of Chartres with its twining streets, its steep lanes and swinging signs; its market stalls and ginger-colored roofs and above all, the majesty of its great cathedral. Now this world was forever changed. That terrifying Friday night, when I finally crept home, my stepfather was waiting to tell me what I knew too well.

"This...*thing, this fire*...it's not happened here for many years," he barked at me. "How did it come to happen now?" His narrow eyes, canny and quick, scanned my face as if to find some explanation stamped there.

Saying nothing, I looked down.

My stepfather, Henri, having had a hard life, liked to make life hard on others. Generally he was wary of neighbors as well as strangers and even coins, which he always bit. Now his wariness fixed on me. The man had been half asleep and drunk when the fire started. But no fool, he.

Henri had just recalled my custom of lighting tapers inside the cathedral on my birthday's eve. Somehow he knew I was not abed when the Night Watch cried *"Fire"* in the streets. The baker's shrewd, crude, cunning mind had sidled toward suspicion, then lurched to certainty.

"We're done if you done what I think you done," he threw his words at me.

With each toss, his right fist struck his left hand. In his voice there was a judgment, fully formed, about the folly of this dreamy female stepchild: me, his cross to bear, as he had often told me.

"What you done." Another spate of hard words; another spate of pictures in my mind....

Cinders falling like black snow and the fire's strange red glow against the sky and the blaze a living thing, breathing, raging and leaping like a demon from roof to roof to roof.

Heat stronger than a summer's noon and behind me, the cathedral's spires rising, pointing, reaching from a moat of fire.

People shouting, horses screaming, children wailing—and then a sudden downpour: drenching sooty rain, saving the town.

"A miracle, a miracle," people crying on their knees, hands raised to the sky, and I am kneeling with them, but they offer prayers of thanks. Mine are only silent pleas for God's mercy and forgiveness....

"I seen no lightning that night," my stepfather cut into my thoughts. "Cecile, you listen to me now. You'll burn next if you had a part in the Great Fire. If anybody knows or thinks you did, mark my words, it's the end of us. At least the Holy Relic wasn't lost—" He crossed himself— "The Blessed Virgin's tunic. My girl, you get down on your benders and thank God for that."

My stepfather brought his face so close to mine I smelled onions and alcohol on his breath. "Never tell me what happened. I don't want to know. Not a word of this at all, you understand me, girl—"

He rapped each word into his hand—"Not to any friend, any priest, any living, blessed soul."

That left the dead and the damned.

A daunting array of confessors, those. And now my shame and fright was so overpowering, I did not even trust the dead—except my gentle mother.

This was not encouraging.

Who would hear me now?

I ruled out the saints, whose standards were no doubt a good deal higher than my mother's; with the blessed I didn't have a chance. Demons, maybe? But they would take no interest in me, a simple baker's daughter

That left the damned.

I must have joined their number already. But before I called on them, I made certain that my stepfather was snoring. Then I ran out into the dark and off to the scene of the disaster. There, speaking clearly, I offered my confession and repentance to the place itself.

At night, the cathedral ruins formed a different, distant country—an immense star that had somehow crashed to earth; a place where time had stopped and history was gone and nothing mattered.

Here I was no longer that guilty Cecile, the baker's daughter; I was but her ghost, unhitched from life and its consequences, at least for a while.

"Take my dearest thing," I raised my voice to no one in particular. "If that would bring the cathedral back again, even grander than before."

I forgot my aunt's warning to be careful what you ask for. Amid the ruins, three nights in a row, I prayed aloud, pacing and confessing. No response. Not even from the damned.

I threw myself on God's promised mercy.

No sign of it. Not one flicker of comfort. Not even a just punishment. No key to working out my own redemption. The Good Shepherd, Christ Himself, seemed silent.

And so, on that third night, I lost whatever hope was left to me. Weakened, it snapped like a frozen branch. I felt that I was falling, plunging, landing in the depths of my own self. On that night, I was certain of this and only this: No one was listening to me.

I gazed at the cathedral's jumbled remains. Then I picked my way across the scattered stones to the South Tower, still standing, solid, pointing at the sky. Its door was open. Inside, the dim stone stairway spiraled upward through the narrow space.

There was a smell of damp and moss and sooty air. The place had the uneasy quiet of a fresh grave. I took a few steps upward. No one barred my way. No heavenly voices called a halt. Bolder now, I moved on, creeping higher, deeper into darkness, one hand on the sweating wall.

Halfway up the stairs, I knew what I must do. When at last I came out into the open belfry, I was doubly certain. In this place, now emptied of bells, I would sacrifice my life to pay for this disaster. Since I was already damned, I thought, how could my suicide matter now?

As I glanced out, the ground appeared to heave and whirl. The cathedral's ruins spread beneath me. Light-headed, I drew back. This perfect penance, as I thought it, would be harder than I had imagined. My inner confusion had made me into a dimwit. How could I forget my fear of heights?

Once more I looked out and once more the earth seemed to pitch toward me at a crazy tilt. My stomach churned and my head seemed to spin; I gripped the stones with damp hands and closed my eyes. The darkness felt solid. The world stopped circling around me. Eyes still closed, I took a breath and leaned out of the tower.

■

You up there," a man called below.

"Let me be," I shouted back.

"Come down— *by the steps.*"

"Go away," I shouted again.

"Why should I, M'amselle?"

My eyes opened; I saw his lamp.

"Who are you to meddle here?" I yelled.

"Who are *you* to do the same?"

"Go now," I lied. "And I'll come down."

There was a long silence.

Maybe he had gone. I no longer saw his light. Who was he? No priest, surely, or he would have invoked his office by now. He had a voice that inked words on the air. Someone from the Cathedral School? I doubted it. No one ever visited this ruined place by night; I'd never spied one figure.

I listened.

Nothing.

Closing my eyes, I leaned out again, smelling rain on the night air. It would be to easier to jump like this, moving blind. No lurching earth, no spinning head. Only this way could I make my leap. I would have to feel for the stone ledge with my eyes closed. For some moments, I stood back against the wall, saying my final prayers. Just in case.

Footsteps sounded on the tower stairs.

"Hold on." The same man's voice.

"Stop where you are," I called.

"*Wait.*" His was closer. "Wait for me."

"I've waited too long—almost."

Now I must be very quick indeed.

Eyes shut, I felt for the belfry's walls and open window ledges but I got turned around. My fingers searched for solid stone and instead found solid flesh: A man's chest, cloaked, and on my shoulders, two restraining hands. I struggled but he was too strong for me. I cursed, kicked out, and upset his lanthorn. It sputtered and went out.

"Grand." The man's tone was wry. "Spiral steps, pitch dark, no light."

"I told you—let me be."

"Let you jump?" His voice was quiet.

"You didn't know that—"

"But I did." I felt his smile against my face. "I've had such passing thoughts right here."

"I never saw you." I tried to pull away.

"But I saw *you*. Three night straight."

"Where were you?" I could not break his hold.

"Nearby. You kept me on the ground."

"And how was that, I might ask?"

"You might. When we're down the stairs."

"That's a bribe." I was stalling now.

"Call it a prediction." He found the steps.

"Why bother with me?" I whispered.

"Why not?" He took my hand.

"A waste of time." I held back.

"Slowly now. And *hold on*."

The tower looked like a deep well.

"Crazy, this," I balked. "Can't do it."

"Crazy, maybe, but we're doing fine."

We felt our way, hand-in-hand, clinging to the tower's walls. Measured steps we took, this shadow of a man and I, working our way down as if we were one person in an upended tunnel.

When he moved, I moved. When he paused, I paused. We drew breath together and together we felt our way down. This became a pattern: he went first, gripping my hand, and I followed in silence.

Step-step-stop-again: *step-step-stop and breathe* —a strange dance it was, with a tall and faceless partner. I was oddly unafraid. I knew the man could be no taverner or thief or vagabond.

He smelled of cinnamon and silk and leather. His voice was low and even; his speech, cultured, and strong were his long hands.

This was someone I had never met—he was not from Chartres, then. All the better. I wouldn't find myself selling him baguettes or sweets at the bakery. Thank God. I would not hear this voice in our shop or see the secret in his eyes.

As I let my thoughts go spinning off, my shoe skidded on slick moss and I slipped down two steps so swiftly I could not catch myself. Suddenly, this stairwell did not seem the perfect place to die. The man held onto me, righted me, and held me where I was.

"You're shaking," he said at last.

"No." I made my voice casual, calm.

"Oh?" He kept a firm grip on my hand.

"I'm perfectly to rights," I told him.

"Well?" He took a step. "Coming?"

"Do I have a choice, M'sieur?"

"Is that a serious question?"

"Is that a serious answer?"

"I like that quality in you."

"What?" I knew. "A saucy tongue?"

"No. I would say...you're spirited."

"I would say you're kind. Or lying."

"That's all the thanks I get?"

"For saving the maiden in the tower?"

"Too trivial. For making me laugh."

Despite the dark, or because of it, our laughter spilled along the steps and echoed and came back to us as we moved down, faster now. Never was I so gladdened by the sight of earth again.

He led me outside and the night seemed to expand around us, dimly lit by that waning moon. It was impossible to see each other plain but we stood staring at each other's silhouettes. His was tall and lean and steady. I wondered if my smaller one wavered like a moth's. We stood silent for a while.

"I do thank you," I said finally. "That, M'sieur is *my* serious answer."

"Don't mention it, M'amselle."

"I just did. And meant it."

He chuckled but said nothing. Stillness hung about him like silken bed-hangings. I could feel his gaze; it had the intensity of sun on a mirror. In his bearing, I sensed lofty rooms and inlaid floors, lutes and books. This was the way of my mother and my aunt who once lived so—*not* my stepfather's way, no matter how prosperous he was. I supposed this unknown man was someone's guest, a visitor. Surely he would drift away and never discover who I was.

"Comfortable, the dark," he said then. "My mother called it 'magic space.' "

"Yes. The dark keeps our secrets."

"Just so." I stared at him so hard my eyes began to sting. "She put it that way."

" 'Magic space.' A secret place to think, to pray, to walk. You need this. As I do."

"How did you know?" I took a step away from him but still he held my hand.

"Nothing to fear." He paused and, when he went on, his speech was halting. "Kept me on the ground, you did, these three nights past."

"I doubt it." I shook my head.

"True. Desperate, trapped, alone: so I felt. Hard to admit." A self-mocking laugh. "No way to tell you what I'm facing now. Escape began to look tempting. Watching you, I felt less alone." He turned to me. "You understand, I think."

I did but was afraid to say so. In fact, I was moved by his confession and, I must admit, not a little flattered. To cover this, I spoke to him in a formal tone. My words were false and fancy, spoken in the feminine manner I always resisted.

"Sir, you are insufferably bold." I thought that sounded rather dashing. "All of this is most improper." Weren't women meant to say such things? "Such conduct is out of keeping." What else could I add? "Maybe daft as well."

"Maybe." He seemed to smile. "Maybe not."

~~~

"Maybe not," I told him the next night among the ruins, as if no time had passed between our meetings and our conversations.

"Agreed." Again he seemed to smile.

Of course I'd known exactly where to find him. I was almost certain he would be there once again. However I hated to admit it, I'd looked forward to seeing him as I moved through the day's tasks. Silly girl, I told myself. Foolish child. Ridiculous.

With my stepfather and his apprentices, I baked, I sliced, I kneaded fresh dough for the next day's pastries and set it out to rise. I sold sixty-nine baguettes and fifty-six sweet rolls that morning but had to do the tally twice. The supper I offered was hasty: pottage, strawberries, and almond milk.

As soon as the household was quiet, I was out the door and off into the night. Scandalous conduct, I told myself and kept on going. Nicolette, the housekeeper, was sleeping in her attic place. My step-father, long in his cups, was now abed.

I had no trouble escaping through the silent, damaged, dreaming town, many of its wooden houses half rebuilt already. I chose a quiet lane and walked faster still. Chartres' rows of tiled roofs seemed to guard me.

When I reached the ruins, I made out the stranger's silhouette. He seemed to face the town, as if searching for someone, and he stood by the cathedral's South Tower, as if to guard its heavy door from any reaching hands. When he saw my outline, he moved toward me.

"Good evening, M'amselle."

"The same to you, M'sieur."

We laughed at our formality.

"Planning yet another climb?"

"Not in the dark," I told him.

"Good. Grand. Wise decision."

"I am in your debt, M'sieur."

"No debt." His angular frame shifted.

"You mean to say you cancel it?"

"Cancel what does not exist?"

I had no saucy retort that time.

"A walk, perhaps?" He suggested.

"On the ground, yes. A walk."

"Strictly on the ground. Good."

"You must know your way about."

"Risky patches here. A maze, this is."

"It seems to be my week for risks."
He offered his arm. "Not with me."
"A stranger in the dark, oh no."
"Another serious answer?"
I took his arm. "This is."

~~~

He was there at the South Tower every night for three weeks, always arriving first and departing last. I did not know where he'd been or where he went and I did not ask. Still he made himself easy to find, even during the dark of the moon.

For hours, each night, we rambled the grounds of the ruined Cathedral, even as it changed; every day workmen were removing more of the scattered and scorched debris.

We walked with care and yes, we watched each other, too, but never directly. The new moon, even as it waxed, gave little light and so we couldn't see each other plain. The man often took my arm, sometimes my elbow; most often, my hand.

"To be safe," he told me.
"Of course," I told him.

The cathedral's great lead roof had melted and caved in. In the starlight we could make out the vague shapes of hanging beams. I still remember the burnt black smell about the place and charred wooden beams that hung about us as we moved and whispered and walked.

This scent clung to my clothes: A sour stench, I thought at first, but somehow it came to be a pleasant aroma, reminding me of those nights when we stepped out of our worrisome worlds; out of the confines of time itself.

We spoke of many things. His fondness for plums. My dislike of plums. His taste for spices; my taste for sweets. Our shared preferences for the color blue and winter dawns and autumn nights. One subject had strict boundaries: a moat we never breached.

Neither of us revealed who we were or what we did during the day. From the stranger's speech, I guessed he was young, Parisian and educated: perhaps a scholar, a musician? I never asked. He never said. From the start, that was our unspoken bargain. And we kept it.

Even so, I knew this man's step, his stride, his laugh, his voice. In some uncanny way, we had grown quite close; decorous and yet familiar with each other. "Dark Friends," my mother would have called us.

" 'Dark Friends,' " I explained to him. "Before she died, my mother told me there were such. I think she had one. Pairs of travelers or lovers, even neighbors, sometimes—folk who only meet at night."

" 'Dark Friends,' " he repeated the term. "Perfect. Good name for the two of us."

"I didn't mean—" My face went hot.

"I know. You're flushing."

"How can you tell?" I asked.

"Call it a hunch," he said.

"Now you're smiling."

"You see that?"

"Call it luck," I said.

"I have. For weeks."

"That means...?"

"I think you know."

We were making up our own language, our own rules, from night to night, and none of it seemed wrong or bad or dangerous. I sensed no sin, no scandal, no shame, though I well knew these meetings might shock anyone else.

"What the hell do you think you're about?" my stepfather would have yelled at me if he knew how I passed my evenings. And I would have no answer, even if I suffered a beating for my silence. I truly didn't know what I was about, or what my "dark friend" was about. One night I asked him.

"Why do we keep coming here?"

"You wonder if it makes sense?"

"Well." I faced him. "Does it?"

"It does to me. And you?"

"Not the ordinary way."

"A different way. Like this."

He took my hand and we began to walk again in widening circles. Perched on scattered stones we talked, we laughed. Each night more rubble was gone and our patterns changed. But he did not change, my "dark friend."

Until the start of the third week.

That was when he turned to me and took my face into his hands. A simple, tender touch was his; I did not want to feel it flickering away. After a moment of hesitation he asked me a question.

"Will you say I am 'insufferably bold'?"

"Now?" I leaned toward him.

He drew me closer. "Now?"

"Not now." I lifted my face to his.

"Now?" He kissed my forehead.

"Not yet." I touched his cheek.

He bent to me and pressed his mouth to mine and we tasted each other for the first time. His lips, firm and soft at once, lingered on my own.

"Ever?" He asked after a while.

"Is that a serious question?"

His laugh was quiet. "Yes."

Before I could answer a lamp glimmered at the ruins' farthest edge. The light seemed to hang in the dark like a stranded moon. Then we heard the old sexton mutter to himself. Motionless, we stayed in our embrace.

"Anybody there?" the sexton called.

Afraid to breathe, I watched his lamp.

The old sexton wheezed and swore.

"The death of me, this place," he spat.

Slowly, his light swung toward us. My companion disappeared in one direction; I crept toward another. We dodged the arc of light in time but now, without a light ourselves, we couldn't find each other.

"Someone's about," the sexton called again. "I been here too damn long, you can't fool me."

I heard him raking the loose gravel with what might have been a stick. "Show yourself, why don't you? Naught for you to find or steal or borrow here. Mark me, now, begone."

I couldn't make out my companion's silhouette nor could I hear his step. What if we got lost in this broad field of rubble and couldn't find each other—or our way? I tripped over something hard and low but did not fall. Even so, I made a small noise.

"Come to rob me, did you?" The sexton's words were thickened by drink, as I expected. "Come to rob old François? You'll not profit by it."

If I could reach the sexton and his light, my comrade might spot my bright hair, but the sexton would see me, too. I tried to think of some excuse for being here at night.

"You a stranger's, maybe?" The sexton raked the gravel once again; he seemed much closer. "The cathedral's gone if that's what you're after." Slurred words, then a gurgling laugh. "You got eyes, you can see that for yourself. Off with you then."

On my hands and knees I felt my way through the rubble. No use tripping over something else. As I neared the sexton, I was still wondering what was best to say. Even though I crept along with quiet care, François looked about. He set his lanthorn on a high, flat rock and shouted.

"If you'll not show yourself to me, I'll show myself to you and I'll be quick about it. You're up to no good, I'd wager, you so deadly silent."

François took a step, caught his foot on a root and fell flat, still near his light. I saw blood on his forehead; he tried but could not rise.

"Oh Jesus God," the old man cried. "Oh Jesus, not again. A month past, You let me fall. My first night back, I'm down again. Lose my job, I will."

Now what? I couldn't leave François and I couldn't find my friend. Bolder, now, I crawled into the sexton's circle of light.

"Are you to rights?" I asked him.

"Stupid question. Who in hell are you?"

"A friend. I was near, I heard you call."

"Get me to my feet, damn it."

"Lean toward me, sir. I'll try."

I stood in the light and glanced around. All I saw was rubble and fallen beams. Now François was sitting up; not badly hurt, I thought. Putting my back into the task, I tried to get him standing. The man appeared small and frail but he was dead weight. I couldn't lift him.

"Forgive me, M'amselle." François grabbed my shoulders, leaned on me and tried again to stand. We both went down—with a crash. The poor man fell onto soft ground and I'm ashamed to say, I fell on him. Rolling away, I knelt, then and stood once more, keeping my face out of the sexton's direct gaze.

"I'll go for help." I raised my voice.

"You think me deaf?" He snapped.

"I want you to hear me," I shouted.

"Jesus God, you'll wake the dead."

"I'm getting help," I called again.

"Here it is." That other voice I knew.

"Thank God." I turned around.

"Amen." My friend was behind me.

"Who in hell—?" François sputtered.

"We'll get you home. You live over there, yes?" My friend lifted François to his feet and, with the lanthorn, we three picked our way through the rubble to François' cell in the North Tower. My "dark friend" took care to turn his head, avoiding the sexton's eyes.

As we settled the old man, François lifted the light and stared straight into my face; I backed off into the shadows then and hoped he would forget me.

"I know you," he stared harder.

"Go to sleep now, M'sieur."

"You don't belong here."

"Rest, sir," my friend said.

"I'll have to tell the Bishop."

"This is all a dream," I added.

"The Bishop. In the morning."

"It was a dream." I was firm.

"I'll be sure to tell the Bishop."

■

Would the sexton tell the Bishop? I fretted all that night. Would the stranger meet me the again? So I wondered throughout the next day. And would I dare meet him? Somehow I knew he would, I would, and when we did there was news to share.

The old sexton was indisposed and might not return to his work. At early mass, François had informed everyone, including the Bishop, that an angel had come to him in a dream last night.

People exchanged knowing looks. Before they could question him, François passed out. We took no joy in such tidings—but we felt safe again.

In fact we were not.

We did not know how close death was to us in our secret world. Even as the waxing moon spilled more light and left us more exposed, we were so drawn to each other, we sensed no peril. Nighttime held our favored hours. Then, I thought, we were most truly awake.

Midway through the third week, the light was brighter and in a sudden flash, I saw the Great Fire in my mind, as if it were happening again—the cathedral blazing like a torch against that eerie crimson sky, the great church caving in upon itself.

To my shame, hot tears stung my face. I wiped my cheeks with both hands and my companion could make out these motions in the darkness.

"You lost a husband here?" He tensed.

"I have no husband."

"A loved one?" He tensed again.

"Not yet." I looked away.

"Ah." He seemed relieved. "Nor I. You mourn the cathedral, then?"

"I can't say. I wish—"

"No matter, let it go."

"This church—" I broke off.

I had grown up in its nave, passing time there while the other children were about their gaming. I felt at ease when I was there alone, safe from my stepfather's temper.

The stained glass and the statues gave me the beauty I craved; the only beauty I had in my workaday world, apart from what I saw in nature.

"But the windows," I confided, "they were what I loved the most. And I'd watch their colored light move across the stone—you think me mad?"

"Not at all. You can't see my face."

"Almost. You want to stay hidden?"

"Makes things simpler, doesn't it?"

He took a step back and with that step, I felt a sudden chill. I had put off an irksome but insistent question. Now this question, held too long, surfaced with surprising force. I drew a breath before I spoke.

"Are you in some kind of trouble?"

"No. And yes." His voice was low.

"What kind?" My tone sharpened.

"Not the kind you might fear."

"And what is that?" I snapped.

"Murder, prison, ravishing maidens—"

"How can you make light of this?"

"That's my way when I'm troubled."

"I asked you before—what trouble?"

"My work. Or rather, the lack of it."

"I'm sorry, I couldn't guess."

"It's only here that I can breathe."

Somewhere above us, I heard the groan of wooden beams; a familiar among the ruins. Nothing ever moved or shifted and, by now, I doubted something would. I ignored the sound; instead, I searched instead for the right words to offer my silent companion.

"You need say nothing more." I began.

"I'm grateful." He paused. "What's wrong?"

"I thought I heard...it's nothing."

Now he was the one who tried to speak, shifting on his feet, gathering his words with care.

"My father, he *was* famous." A short silence. "Famous for his work, the same as mine. In Paris. Beyond. Makes it harder for an only son. A son who must perform. Or fail." He turned away from me. "The pressure grows. It's almost unbearable."

"You, too, need a 'magic space.'"

"Yes. Since my mother's death, I closed up tight as a fist." His voice was quiet, like a leaf afloat on a still pond. "Some call me cold. But my work needs warmth. This I have but cannot reach."

"I've come to know you well," I told him. "And I believe your reach is longer than you think."

"Here I feel that. With you."

Again, I heard the sound of shifting wood. Where was it? I could not see what was just above us. In any case, the creaking stopped.

"What of you, when your mother died?"he asked after some hesitation. "I doubt *you* closed up."

"Me, no," I dared to say. "I wanted a new love, but not the kind you hear about in ballads." I seemed to pluck words from the dark, as if it were a field of wild black flowers. "Raw love, real—you're laughing?"

"Never." He stepped closer. "When you speak that lively heart of yours, I remember when I felt alive. Easy to forget. When one is alone."

"You're not alone now."

He pulled me against him; his mouth seemed to drink me in. This kiss was harder, deeper, thirstier than before. I heard nothing for a time: No sound of shifting beams—until it was almost too late. I drew back, listening.

"What?" He whispered.

"Wait. Hear that?"

It came again, that sound, louder now, and though I could not see the falling beam, I sensed where it was. No time for words—I grabbed my "dark friend's" arms and pulled him toward me fast, so fast, we were slipping falling, rolling away from the rafter that crashed onto the space where, moments before, we were standing.

It was only moments, I suppose, but it seemed a long time. We lay trembling there, his body on top of mine, the two of us pressed together. I breathed with him and he with me and we stopped shaking.

Beneath my fingers, I could feel the whole geometry of his back, his shoulder blades and spine. We clung to each other long after that beam had crashed down.

Finally we stood, found our footing, shook ourselves and asked at the same time, in the same urgent voice, if the other was hurt. We were not. He led me then to higher, firmer ground.

"Now I'm in *your* debt," he said.

"No debt." My voice cracked.

"What is it? Tell me. What?"

"That beam," I blurted out. "That beam was meant for me—and only me."

"No." He ran his thumb along my cheek, as if to erase my tears. "Why think it so?"

"I'm ashamed." I took a breath.

"That beam wasn't for you."

"You don't know—"

"Let me hear—"

"I can't—" I choked. "I was part of something bad, unspeakable, and now I can't undo it and—"

I broke off. There was a long silence.

"And you've borne this all alone." With his fingers, he wiped my wet face.

"Who could I tell?" I let out my breath. "The town would string me up if anybody knew."

"The town won't know."

"If *anybody* knew—"

"I do." He paused. "*I* know."

"How?" Stung, I spun around.

"Not by plan. I overheard..."

"You know about my fire?"

"That fire did *not* swallow the cathedral. I was there, had to be, a job. The poor sexton helped me quench the tapers. No need for them to haunt you."

I did not believe him. All I saw was this: my three nights praying aloud, pacing in the ruins, confessing what I'd done. All that time, he heard every word I spoke. And me? I was so distraught I never saw him. Now I felt naked, betrayed, ashamed. When I spoke again, my voice was sharp, accusing.

"You listened to my prayers."

"Yes, in a way, I did."

"Private words." My voice cut.

"You prayed aloud."

A space seemed to snap open between us.

"You let me think you never knew."

"Wrong of me. Shouldn't have."

"Why did you?" I stepped back.

"I feared you'd pull back like this."

"I'm afraid?" Another step away.

"Nothing to fear from me."

"You might tell what you heard."

"Never. Nor did you cause—"

"How can I believe that?" I was a tree losing its leaves. "How can I believe anything you say?"

"Why not? I give my word of honor."

I could make no answer and I knew he expected one. We had never broken off like this before. The night's crickets sounded loud and querulous for the first time and the air was too close, too warm. I could feel my fear. I could feel his wish.

The fear was winning.

Now the silence spread between us like a field, too wide, too overgrown to cross. The magic of the place, its darkness, his darkness—all at once, it fell away.

Who was he, this man, to give his word of honor? And why was I so pliable, so trusting? I was not bound to him nor he to me. I had simply been enchanted by my first tryst, my first kisses. This would be the end of my youth and foolishness.

At least this man knew little about me: only my voice. Otherwise he could destroy my reputation. Was I crazy? A girl alone, night after night, with a strange man in a dim and lonely place—hearing this, who might think me innocent? My stepfather? He would kill me.

I wheeled around.

And fled.

I leapt from the dim ruins, landing on both feet in the lit and level world again, where I was again myself, the Cecile I knew, with tarts to glaze and hair to braid and sheets to wash.

No more magic places for me, no more dark spaces or dark friends—notions for silly girls. I would blot out this odd interlude and this man from every memory I had.

I would never think of him again.

I would never listen for his voice.

I would never miss these nights.

Maybe he would move on with his work and that would be the end of it. He could travel to another town and, for all I knew, talk to other strange girls in the dark.

I kept to our bakery by day, except when I went to market or, rarely, to deliver pastry. At night, I stayed at home, did the mending, doused the oil lamps early and was soon abed. But dull routine did not dull my thoughts as I had hoped. Against my will, I wondered if the stranger waited.

Twisting in my sheets, I lulled myself to sleep by chanting every recipe for every kind of bread and cake and tart I knew. In my mind, I counted crocks of honey in the larder. I went through our entire inventory at least seven times.

After a while, I would drift into an uneasy slumber and wake before dawn, to help bake that day's fresh bread. The familiar smells of dough and yeast hung all about me once again. I scoured my clothes to rid them of the ruins' smoky scent. Never would I savor it nor anything about this strange month of June. Never would I see that man again. Never could I guess how wrong I was.

■

I heard. I sneaked. I spied.

I saw him one week later in the Bishop's Palace on the night of a great feast.

My confession is this: I was peering down at the banquet hall through a small hole in the floor above: it lay next to the main bedchamber, or solar, as we called it. To me, this space was a familiar perch. It was mine whenever I was at the palace —more often than you might suppose.

The Bishop was a generous host; he loved to entertain and did it often, did it well. I was always called upon to provide bread and pastries for one occasion or another. Sometimes I even served—and I knew what all servants discover:

Even Bishops' palaces have mice and mold; knotholes and floorboards that do not quite meet. As a child, I often watched the glimmering cracks in our bedchamber's floor, lit from the room below. I would gaze at those ribbons of light until I fell asleep.

Magical, they looked to me then. Tempting, they looked to me now: vantage points for secret sightings. My fear of heights was stilled because the floor itself was strong and broad.

Had it given way, I would have plummeted headfirst through the fragranced air when I first heard that voice below—the stranger's voice. The stranger from the ruins; the voice of my "dark friend."

I listened closely, not quite believing he could be so near, so suddenly. I hoped I was wrong; I hoped I was right. I put my ear against the knothole. Not good enough. I crawled across the floor to a find better listening post and there I listened once again.

There was no denying it.

That was the same voice I had heard for two dozen nights amid the cathedral's ruins: I knew its varied tones, its cadence, its pitch. It was the voice that called, "Wait for me" and said so firmly, "I am in your debt." This voice confided secret fears and told old jokes and made me laugh when laughter seemed almost impossible.

Now I was breathless at my discovery—there he was, just below me in the brightness of the Bishop's great hall, at the most impressive banquet I had ever witnessed. I hid behind my server's role at most of Chartres' celebrations, but this one surpassed all.

Who could count the jewels and the silks fluttering below me? The wealthy and powerful were always at grand events but on this night, there were guests from Venice and Madrid and Rome, as well as Paris. All of them, of course, were desirable donors for the new cathedral's building fund.

I thought of Chartres, that night, as the center of the European world. Perhaps, that night, it was. The Holy Father had a keen interest in raising another great pilgrimage cathedral. In fact, a Papal Legate was rumored to be present just below. Not to mention architects, sculptors and glaziers, all vying for commissions. Not to mention the Count of Chartres, himself.

There was no greater call for funds, for craftsmen, for designers, and patrons with deep coffers of gold. I knew no one like that. Perhaps my "dark friend" would turn out to be a musician as I'd guessed. Otherwise, this did not seem the right setting for him. Or for me.

And why, you may well wonder, was I present at such a grand feast? The reason was simple:

Bread.

We baked it and we brought it. My stepfather, that fox, had maneuvered another sort of commission for himself and our shop.

A great honor, this: Provision of all baked goods, including *patisserie*, crowned by an immense and showy centerpiece as dessert and decoration—a replica of the Bishop's Palace, designed and sculpted and glazed by me, the would-be artist.

For days I had labored to craft that monstrous palace, meant to be the banquet's *piece de resistance*. But something always went wrong at these events. Every time. Without exception. Some detail would catch fire, fall apart, or run out.

I hoped my elaborate creation would survive until it was presented—if no one dropped it, sat on it, or nibbled it. God forbid. I slapped away the greedy hands of servants who were trying hard to "pinch the palace."

In most cases, though, servants know the truth: depend on it. We are expert eavesdroppers. Hire us and we will overhear the latest, ripest facts: who had mistresses and who did not, who had money, who did not, who had both or would and generally in what amounts.

Tonight, the talk ran to the men competing for the new and coveted commissions: the Master of Works, chief architect of the new cathedral; the Master of Masons and Sculpture; and the Master Glazier of 176 new stained glass windows.

The rumor was that Jacques Bonnet would be awarded the greatest prize: Master of Works. Bonnet, a fleshy red-faced man, was famed as a great architect, an expert in sacred geometry—often called a genius but a humble one. His genius outweighed his reputation as an active lover.

The sculptural Master, Paul Épars, had several powerful sponsors and, according to irreverent gossipers, a secret mistress. As for the Master Glazier, there were two contenders; one man, Gabriel Larue, was under special scrutiny. No tasty rumors about him; what a disappointment to us.

Still on the rise, not quite twenty-three, he was highly regarded for his work in France, not only as a Master Glazier but a glass-painter as well: two gifts rarely combined. That was all anyone could say. No one knew which one he was in the throng downstairs. Perhaps tonight we would learn his name, at least.

Trumpets sounded to announce more guests, new wine, and the jugglers who entertained before most feasts. Their shining batons and balls, tinted gold and silver, seemed to rise just out of our reach. Tonight they did not hold my gaze.

I had come here with one obsession:

Baked dough.

Its quantities. Its freshness. Its reception.

Toward the end of the feast, I would be called downstairs to present our sweets—an ordeal I dreaded. Perhaps I could stay hidden and avoid that appearance before the guests.

But I was no mouse to cower here. The stranger from the ruins did not know my name or trade or looks—only my voice. I would remain nameless, then, invisible and totally, constantly, absolutely mute.

Looking back now, I see myself as I was that night: kneeling on the floor of that storeroom where I am suspended like a rehearsing acrobat In the storeroom's dimness, vague shapes lurk behind me: bins and barrels stacked against one wall.

I see a slender young woman, her curling red hair concealed by a white cloth, her skirt and tunic covered with an equally white apron, stiff with starch. She resembles a peak of stiffly whipped cream rather than a girl.

There she crouches, peering through those cracks and holes in the old floor. Like sleek fish in a chateau's garden pond, the guests appear to swim beneath her where they glide and bow and sashay to show off their finery—silks the colors of blood and butter and brandy.

The hall is lit with hundreds of expensive beeswax candles, tall and white as lily stalks, while handfuls of rose petals are scattered down by servants throughout in the great hall. There is laughter and light and a sense of promise, greed, and strain.

Why is that? The gossips speculate but no one is quite sure as we look down on this celebration. Feasts are our entertainments, all without expense to us, and this is the best one we have seen—until later, when the fighting starts.

I feel the fight already in the air.

It will not be a peaceful evening.

■

C olor!" It is a shout. "More color!"

Now I look down on a balding head set atop a huge hill of a man, flanked by two strong arms and enormous splayed hands: strong hands, gifted hands; a stone mason's hands.

"More color, more light, I say."

The speaker cuts his meat with such power and precision that I know, even before he is addressed, this is Jacques Bonnet, the man certain to be chosen as Master of Works, the architect of this daring cathedral.

A mason's son, renowned as a genius, he has raised many fine churches. Bonnet is known for his superior knowledge of sacred geometry, his dead-straight plumb lines and his skill at measuring with compass pincers.

"In my design," the mason waves the skewered meat, "we build higher than ever before—and we build wider, opening the walls to make them *walls of stained glass.* We support the whole with layered columns and with flying buttresses."

The Bishop looks a challenge at the powerful Abbot Claude Chevan, whose thin face has darkened like a sky before a hailstorm. "No, Sir," he cries.

"Yes!" The Bishop raises his voice. "Gothic is the coming thing. This style that allows in more of God's light to lift the soul in prayer."

"*Distracts* the soul," Chevan snaps.

"Father Abbot, I beg to differ."

"Beg? No use, your Excellency."

"Let us speak cordially—"

"Don't challenge me, then."

"I stand with M'sieur Glazier."

"I stand against you both."

The air below is turning sour as a jug of curdled milk. This is not how things are meant to go, I know. The company is not yet through the first course and already there is argument. It has a nasty edge to it, this talk, each word a blade.

A flight of doves intervenes.

A sign, some servants whisper.

These doves bear no olive branches in their beaks but their arrival has an amazing effect: a temporary truce. The doves' presentation appears nothing less than Providential.

Released into the Bishop's Great Hall, a dozen birds rise from a newly opened pie, the size of a wagon wheel and borne by four lads. They are very much alive, these doves, not baked into that pastry crust but trapped beneath it.

I know this for a fact.

I stuffed that pie.

I wouldn't eat it.

Now, with thrumming wings, the doves fly upward and dart about the room, passing in and out of sight; at last they range themselves along the rafters. We laugh as all the ladies dodge away from any patch of floor beneath these creatures.

" '... *four and twenty blackbirds were baked into a pie...*'" I whisper the old children's rhyme. "Is that the notion? '*When the pie is opened the birds begin to sing...Isn't that a tasty dish to set before a king?*'"

Nicolette, my comrade, is always the realist.

"Ah no," she whispers back. " '*...four and twenty white doves baked into a trap.... When the trap is opened the birds begin to crap.... Isn't that a tasty topping for a Bishop's hat?*'"

"Oh Nic, no, not here."

"So they sing in the kitchen."

"Couldn't be, the doves were starved."

"Cecile, more than petals will drop tonight."

A trumpet fanfare startles me, as well as Nicolette, our housekeeper, kneeling beside me in the storeroom. Two years my senior, she is sister, confidante and friend to me—a bold girl, a beauty with dark hair that coils around her head like some exotic snake.

The daughter of a bankrupt silk merchant, she was forced to go into domestic service and this,

I know, is still a source of pain and anger to her, except on occasions like this one.

Tonight, she draws on her late wealthy life for information on the guests below. Nicolette's commentary makes her the center of attention up here in the storeroom and she relishes her role.

"Look, the Papal Legate, most impressive." Nicolette taps the floorboard sharply with a finger. "The Holy Father's chosen agent here. Ah, look now. The Count of Chartres and his Countess. And I see Jean Morrisot—the Bishop's brother. Look, he's there, right there."

She taps the floor again. I see a wintry man, perhaps fifty, a bit gaunt but striking. Surrounding him is a swaying cluster of long silken tunics.

"Arrogant, crafty, they say," Nic goes on about him now. "Outspoken. Older. Powerful...and oh so wealthy. Collects art."

"Wealthier than the Bishop?" I ask.

"Ah, yes. Morrisot trades in silks and spices..." She leans closer and whispers. "...from Venice, Florence, Spain. Imagine." Nic smiles. "Better yet, he is a widower...an eligible man. A grand match for me, don't you think?"

"Marry him, Nic, you'd outdo those flirts."

"I wish. Gets his own way, that one."

"The man talking now...." I put my ear to another crack and hear the voice of my "dark friend" again. Greeting someone, he keeps his tone polite but distant. As he meets others, he speaks in that same courteous but detached way. Introductions are preceding but the exact names are out of earshot.

"Whose voice is that, Nic, do you know?"
"Let me look, which one? Oh *mon Dieu.*"
Dove droppings splash the Abbot's head.
"Extravagance," he shouts at the Bishop.
"The dove's gift?" His Excellency counters.
"Yours." The Abbot snarls. "*This banquet.*"
Again I shift my position, crawling across the rough floorboards, until I am crouching over an immense table: almost U-shaped, with one side open, it allows the servers to move in and out. The table is set so the diners' silken backs may graze the walls; all guests will be facing outward.

The damask tablecloths have a pearly sheen and hang lower on the diners' side, where the cloth serves as one long common napkin. I don't envy those who will have to launder it. Thank God that is not my work tonight.

I check each placesetting, arranged around a trencher made of our thick bread, strong and large enough to serve as a plate. Humbler folk like us *eat* these juice-soaked trenchers. Knives glint beside the goblets and glowing empty bowls. I note the flower garlands on the table and I count our trenchers one more time.

It is then I hear my "dark friend's" voice again: it runs like a low and steady note of music under many bright plucked strings. Brief replies, still polite; nothing more than that.

I know him well enough to guess: This scene gives him no pleasure. He is here as a courtesy or as a duty. I scan the hall as best I can.

"Nic, who's that man, look there."

"Which one? Ah, now it begins."

Yet another trumpet fanfare calls the guests to take their seats. I find myself looking directly down upon a silken cap, tufted roundabout with graying well-trimmed hair:

His Excellency, the Bishop himself—a man of kindness, amiable but ambitious; longing, it is said, to change his purple hat for a cardinal's red one. To his right, that figure of great importance: the Papal Legate. Now the Bishop gathers up his plum-colored robes and stands.

He blesses the guests.

He blesses the feast.

He blesses the town.

He blesses France.

Then, in his dignified voice, he proclaims, "Tonight, we answer one miracle with another. Chartres' sacred relic draws Europe's finest citizens to make a new miracle here. The greatest cathedral ever seen will rise at Chartres in one generation."

Goblets lift.

Cheers rise.

Candles shine.

More gitterns are strummed and strolling minstrels sing. A merry company it seems, indeed. And certainly a wealthy one, which is to the Bishop's purpose: everyone, from lackey to lord, understands that. But I sense how fast this scene could shatter.

"Damn and blast," I mutter.

My view is blocked by the Master Chef, still wearing his toque, who takes great pride in announcing the banquet's first course: a Cockentrice, supposed to be a magical beast, not unlike a unicorn.

Unless you've seen it in the kitchen. The thing is a capon's head and breast stitched to a pig's body, designed to look like one beast. It never fails to disgust me. It never fails to make a grand impression on everyone else. But the greater impression, that night, is made by words: hard, pointed, sharp.

"Colored light," The Bishop shouts again.

"*Too much color.*" Abbot Chevan rises from his seat. Once he was a soldier, I heard, and a fierce one. That part of him, it seems, hides in his monastic robes. I see a rod of a man with hollow cheeks and veins bulging in his neck.

"Color in a church is vanity." His voice could blister skin. "Like a painted harlot, color is seductive. It draws our admiration, even veneration. Color lures the soul away from God."

Beneath me, the Bishop's fingers drum the table. He is fast losing control of this gathering and he knows it. His voice takes on a honeyed tone.

"Let there be no quarrels here. Leave that to the rest of France, all those 'colorphobes' and 'colorphiles.' No quarrels here at Chartres."

"Color is abused—and *extravagant*. Have you any idea of its expense?" Chevan's voice is louder; I see his hands form fists. "And you want *still* more windows, crammed with colored pictures?"

"Color is worth the expense when it comes to our cathedral," the Bishop roars. "Chartres must glow like a jewel. We will raise the needed monies."

"What of the hungry?"the Abbot shouts. "Will color feed them? Or will it merely turn the cathedral into an entertainment?"

"Didn't the great Abbot Suger choose color for the windows at St. Denis in Paris?" Jean Morrisot's voice slices the air. He points his knife at Abbot Chevan. "Did Sugar not write that light conveys the Divine Essence?"

"*God's* light, plain light." I see the Abbot's spit spray out; his fist strikes the table. "*Grisaille* windows, pure gray. These filled our churches for decades. *Grisaille*. Not colored light."

"Isn't color everywhere in God's world?"

I know that voice. Familiar. Too familiar: the voice that inks words on the air amid the ruins of the old cathedral. *Wait for me. Hold on.* I hear all he ever said to me in one long rush.

To glimpse the speaker, I creep along the floor, crane my neck and peer through yet another crack. Now he is almost directly beneath me. I see his hair, the light brown of chestnut bark. I see firm shoulders, an angular frame; long fingers turning his goblet in endless circles.

When he moves his head, I note a keen gray gaze like sun-washed stone, a square chin and a serious face. He sits straight and poised but I can sense his tension; muscles flex in his strong jaw.

"My father's colors moved the soul in his own work," he says now. "At Chartres, I may use some of his ideas—but I have my own."

My chest tightens. I lie flat on the wooden floor and, squinting, I watch my "dark friend" through the largest knothole in the storeroom's floor.

"Your father—God rest his soul—gave you a fine education and fine training, my son."

The Bishop's goblet is refilled and raised.

"You are still quite young, Gabriel Larue. A rising star, we might say. I admire your work, of course. It graces many churches as well as your restorations at St. Père, here in Chartres."

Hearing this, I stare. I have spent many hours gazing at St. Père's stained glass from inside the church and outside as well. There my love of color was always stirred and fed at once. A glass-painter myself, I admired the details as well.

"You, too, have gifts, we hear." The Bishop nods at Gabriel Larue. "But you must prove them to us, sir." The Bishop smiles and yet his tone is challenging. "Can anyone surpass your father? Can you pass our tests? *That* remains to be seen."

I freeze. This is what the stranger spoke of in the ruins: the son following the famous father; the father who could not be matched. *The pressure grows.* I crawl to yet another vantage point to see more of this man. His name, Gabriel, suits him.

He has that stillness I remember, like silken bed-hangings. A tall man, even seated. But I knew this as we walked in the cathedral's ruins. Quite young, the Bishop calls him, but Gabriel's bearing is that of a mature man who knows his way about the world.

That voice also brings to me the darkness of the ruins and our laughter in the South Tower. My tears slid over those long fingers. That straight back, covered in fine silk tonight, has a landscape I well remember.

Trumpets blare once again, announcing a new course. Out comes a stuffed swan, wings and tail spread wide, borne by two strong men. Now, no swan can impress me or distract me. The gigantic bird floats out of sight and out of mind. My attention stays fixed on Gabriel Larue.

"Which colors would *you* have, sir?" Chevan issues a new challenge. "Tell us, M'sieur Le Glazier. Name your own selections. You have your favorites, your choices, no doubt."

"All colors." It is the quiet voice I know. "But as the central color, I choose—blue. Blue as the favored background. A blue never seen before, one that bathes the sanctuary and the soul."

"Blue?"

"*Blue?*"

"BLUE?"

One word with many voices, shocked, amazed, speaking it, repeating it. What a stir caused by a single color's name. You would have thought Gabriel Larue had leapt upon the table and cried out "*Turks! Whores! Dragons!*"

"Blue, of course," I murmur to myself. The right shade would create quite an effect. We had talked about this color and I feel absurdly pleased that Gabriel Larue champions it. Am I the only one?

Below, there is a brief and brittle silence. Even the clink of crockery and cutlery has ceased; the doves themselves are still. Hands pause in midair. The banquet, for the moment, jerks to a sudden halt.

"Blue is somewhat...*new*." The Bishop turns his goblet in his hand. "A century old or two, I think, here in our French churches. Abbot Suger used blue. This may be all to the good. With it, we show initiative and innovation. Blue has an uplifting savor to it, does it not?"

"I believe it does, Your Excellency," the familiar voice goes on, level but still tense. "You saw blue at Chartres in the famous window of Our Lady." He pauses. "I want to find a different blue, not yet seen or imagined."

"A *newer* blue?" Again Abbot Chevan's hand strikes the table, causing knives and bowls to jump. "A *pretty* color? Perhaps to be in fashion? This, *this*..." he draws a wheezing breath. "This is your choice, sir? Would you make our cathedral into a novelty?"

"I would say...'incomparable.' " Gabriel Larue's tone is dry. "Not the same as novelty, I think."

The hall is still, so still that I can hear the sputter of the candles and the clinking in the kitchen and the mice within the walls. I even hear the Bishop's heavy breathing just below me.

"Blue is no mere fashion." The Bishop has certainty in his voice. "It has come to be Our Lady's sacred color after centuries of dismal black. Blue rises in our incense at the Mass and floats above us in the heavens, does it not?"

"You oppose me?" Chevan explodes.

The Bishop's keen eyes narrow. "Our cathedral should indeed be *non pareil,* incomparable. Let you seek this blue, M'sieur Larue. That is—if you can find it. Only then can we decide aright."

"I would sponsor a cathedral bathed in such a color. It would remind us of God's loving gaze." Morrisot's voice cuts in. He stands there like an autumn oak, losing its dark leaves. "I would sponsor that if—and I mean 'if'—such a color does exist. I would demand solid proof."

"No sir, no." Chevan lifts his bone-white bowl above his head. And then, in what seems one long tumbling fall, he hurls it to the floor, where the bowl shatters—fragments flying out like broken teeth. The crash echoes through the silent hall.

Pointing to the broken crockery, Chevan lets his voice crack like whip. "This is what will happen if you play with color—all of you. And your precious windows. Idolatry, ruins."

His gaze rakes the Bishop and the glass-maker and the assembled company and then, with a measured tread, Abbot Chevan sweeps out of the Great Hall, followed by his monks, one of them glaring like a hellish fiend at Gabriel Larue.

■

C ecile. Hurry. Now."
        Nicolette is prodding me.
"It's time. Past time. Go down there."
    Into that strained silence, into that sour air, I must now step in to proffer sweets. Could there be a worse moment to smile over an array of tarts and candied almonds?
    Likely not. What I dread most is my appearance in the hall. Gabriel Larue has seen me in dim light, true enough, but some light, all the same. Will he recognize me, this man known by the famous and the powerful? They would believe any ruinous rumors Gabriel Larue might pass along.
    I snatch one more look below.
    The stewards are pouring more wine in every goblet in the room and a buzz of voices starts to rise. My knees feel weak and watery as Nic and I descend the servants' backstairs.

"You go out to the guests," I tell her. "Present the sweets. I'll stay in the pantry and ready the next round. You'll do it up just right and I can manage things in here."

The pantry, warm and bright, is crowded with servers. I line them up as they lift trays of glowing berry tarts, glazed in reds and greens—and *blues.* The assistants wait for Nic to lead the procession. She scans the lads for sticky fingers.

"You taste—you die," she warns.

"Now," I direct her. "Slowly, slowly..."

There she goes in my place: Nicolette carries a long tray of sweets and she smiles, dimpling, at the Bishop, Larue and Morrisot. Twice more she makes her way around the hall with our confections. Nic, sometimes a bit too forward, is ever the coquette.

Let her be so—no matter.

At this moment, I am grateful for her ways and for her poise as well. The presentation meets with delighted applause. Nicolette, flushed and pleased, returns to the pantry. I take off my apron, sigh with relief and turn away. It is then I hear the Bishop's voice and it demands my presence.

"Let the author of these delights make an appearance and receive her due credit."

"Cecile," Nicolette elbows me. "His Excellency calls for you, go out. Are you deaf? *Vite.* Quick!"

"Tell him—"

"What? You're hiding in the kitchen?"

"Tell him—"

"What's wrong with you? Go *now.*"

"Tell him—"

"Need I slap you? Don't be a child."

I am called again and there is nothing to be done—I must appear. I remove the cloth from my hair. I watch the tips of my shoes moving, one ahead of the other, beneath the hem of my long green skirt. It seems to take a hundred steps to get from the pantry to the center of the Great Hall.

It opens out around me like a lake I must wade into, slowly, carefully, or I will drown in it. I see the guests around the giant table, with its many leaves, and I see all those faces turn toward me. One of them is the face of Gabriel Larue, I know, but the whole scene blurs before my eyes.

Now, on their shoulders, four men carry in my centerpiece —the huge white replica of the Bishop's palace, sculpted as requested. "Marvelous," guests whisper. Monstrous, I think. As I follow in its wake, my chin lifted, my eyes straight ahead, I make every effort to keep breathing.

Am I proud?

Not tonight.

Am I pleased?

Not in the least.

I only hope to curtsy, turn and run. And so I bob and back away, trying not to trip or tread upon the hem of my skirt, while the company exclaims over my work. Everyone is looking at the palace made of pastry. Almost everyone, that is. I sense another gaze directed at me. I look up and I meet Gabriel Larue's gray eyes.

His guarded face becomes an open doorway.

All at once, I remember. I have seen this man before, in daylight, long before I heard his voice in the cathedral's ruins.

And he has noticed me before. I know this for certain now. The banquet hall fades and I am seeing that past scene: a clearing in the forest where a traveling studio of glass-maker's.

I saw him first through smoke and grass.

Tall grass. Tall plumes of smoke and steam.

I saw him in the forest only two years past: a man with a troupe of other glass-makers, moving, I thought then, like spirits in a haunted grove.

In a clearing, he stood like a magician before a cauldron, and in his hand, a wand—his blow-pipe, of course.

Behind him, a hut with a firepit and ovens shaped like beehives; ovens so powerful I feel their heat, even from a distance.

I knew about the traveling bands of glass-makers in the forest—folk respected as artisans, mistrusted for their unsettled ways.

These men, I realized, must be making staining glass windows from sand and from the ashes of the beech trees all around them.

I came several times to watch the men and once, when the clearing emptied, I ventured toward a shed.

When I stepped inside I saw this man. He stood drawing, I thought, on a high table. I stared at him and he looked up.

That day his eyes were the color of rain clouds. He smiled at me and went back to his work. When I returned another day I watched him. We never spoke. I watched him watching me....

Now, at the banquet, Gabriel Larue is watching me with that same amused gray gaze. There are no trees to hide me now, nor darkness, nor secrecy. I can no longer make myself invisible.

The vast Great Hall feels too small, too hot, too bright, and as the Bishop speaks his praise, I feel as if the walls are closing in. Even Jean Morrisot is watching me with narrowed eyes.

I nod and bob in silence.

"You see how cunningly our famed *patissier* has replicated my palace—and my private chapel. Note, my friends." The Bishop's voice has a steely ring. "She has tinted its windows red, green, *and* that controversial color: *blue*. A perfect likeness, this."

Laughter then and more applause.

"What's your secret, you amazing girl?"

I murmur something no one hears.

"Speak up now. You see," he sweeps his hand across the air as if he owns it. "We have many kinds of native talent here in Chartres. M'amselle, kindly tell my guests who you are."

I am done, doomed, finished. I must make an answer to the Bishop and this time my voice must be heard—on command. I take a breath, straighten my shoulders and step forward.

"I am...nobody," I blurt out.

Laughter. This is taken as a joke.

"Come, my girl, speak your name."

There is a pause before I obey.

"I am Cecile Dufort, the baker's daughter."

Applause resounds throughout the hall.

Gabriel Larue's eyes remain on me.

The Bishop makes a toast.

"M'amselle Cecile Dufort."

"Yes, Your Excellency."

"Make a model of our new cathedral."

"The cathedral?" I stare in surprise. "Your Excellency, an honor." A horror, I am thinking. "But surely, these great masters here need no model, no advice from me."

There. Gabriel Larue has heard my voice and my name and he will now fit the pieces together.

"I would be pleased to see such a model," Jacques Bonnet, quite drunk, raises his goblet to me. "It would be faster and far easier to bake one than to make one out of plaster. But what says the contender for the post of Master le Glazier, I wonder? Gabriel, my friend, speak your thoughts."

I look up at the man who had, just a week before, rolled away from death with me clasped in his arms. Now his gaze has changed; it no longer holds amusement, as before. Something else is there but this I cannot read.

"I give my word of honor." Gabriel speaks directly to me. "I, too, hold you in esteem, M'amselle."

"Enough of this." A sword-like voice commands the company's attention. The Bishop's brother stands at his host's left hand and waves away our banter.

"Think, men. Think." Morrisot goes on. "We are staking our wealth and reputations on this dream: A cathedral where heaven and earth may meet. We speak of windows rising over twenty feet, perhaps with thirty panels each. This is no trifling matter."

He swings the table out so he can step forward and stalk across the room to my "dark friend."

"You promise much, M'sieur Gabriel." The voice of Morrisot is chilling. "Can *you* design on such a scale? Moreover, can you catch God's loving gaze in colored light? Dare you try?"

"I dare you to allow it."

"You? Dare me?" Morrisot snaps.

"I do." Gabriel's voice stays level.

A gasp around the hall, a deeper hush.

Morrisot waits in silence for a moment. I glance at this tall and narrow man: unsmiling, arrogant indeed, with a knife of a nose and eyes like glinting coins. Instantly, I decide I hate him.

"Can you do this thing?" Morrisot challenges Gabriel Larue. "You are cold by nature, it is said."

How rude, I think. How brazen. This man, the Bishop's brother, is so sure of his own power.

"You keep to yourself, I hear," the chilly voice continues. "No engagements, no attachments. If you have not known love, how can you reflect God's love for us? Even a glimpse of it? In glass?"

There is a brittle silence.

"I wonder that you try to provoke me, sir." With effort, Gabriel keeps his tone even. "My private life has no bearing on my work. "You need not squint into my soul."

"I disagree, sir." Morrisot snarls. "A soulless creation is empty skill. What would kindle you to capture God's love in glass? And where will you find this blue you tout? I repeat: does it even exist?"

"It waits for me." Gabriel Larue can also nail words to the air. "The new windows will 'gaze' as you desire. So I pledge."

The Bishop starts a patter of applause that grows and swells and breaks the tension in the air. More wine is poured and more consumed. More sweets are offered and selected. More rose petals are scattered through the hall.

From the center of the room I watch Gabriel, now encircled by well-wishers. Over their heads, he looks at me and I look back at him. To me, our shared gaze is as visible as one long strong thread.

A hundred images are passing through my mind, and his, perhaps. The tower, the ruins, the falling beam, the touch of hands and lips. And so we stand there motionless, he and I, apart and yet connected, while the guests joke and drink and jostle one another—and consume my palace.

■

W elcome to Hell."
So I muttered to myself in our bakery, the morning after the feast. Had it really happened? Perhaps to someone else. In the hour before dawn, I was back where I belonged: in our stone cellar, its walls red and rippling with fire, its air wavering with our ovens' heat.

Often working underground, always among flames, bakers are sometimes thought to be in league with Hell's master—the Devil himself. From time, to time, we are questioned about sorcery and some unfortunates, so charged, have been hanged.

Images of our patron, St. Honoré, are always in plain sight downstairs, upstairs, inside, outside, and on our signboard, along with our other great patron, St. Luke. Sorcery and alchemy are not words we like.

And what is this alchemy we practice?

Not so very different from the alchemy of sand and ash combined and heated until it forms glass, I think, though we work on a far humbler scale. I thought of Gabriel Larue. Again. Had we really seen each other last night, named, and in the light? Looking back at it, the Bishop's banquet seemed to spread around some other Cecile, not me.

Oiling my hands, I rolled out the pastry dough we'd worked the day before and left to rise in dozens of jute baskets, kept on shelves around the walls.

Mixing flour and water, I prepared still more dough for still more bread. Then the kneading: fold and pull, rock and push, that strange rhythm of the working baker.

Irksome dough was what I had that morning. It felt like thick wet rope under my strong fingers, fighting off my touch. Now, with floured hands, I stood at our high tables where I had to work faster.

I twisted dough, I braided dough, I cursed at dough—and all the while I thought of the cathedral ruins in the dark. How childish, how craven I had been to panic and give up those nights, I scolded myself, thumping the resistant stuff before me.

The morning dawned flat and hot. The dough still rebelled. Flour dust began to rise; so did the heat. A batch of baguettes came out blackened. The shop door's string of bells jingled upstairs. This was life—no dream.

My stepfather cast me a sharp look: a clear command to answer the door. I wiped my hands on my apron and took off the cloth around my hair. The bells gave another ring. Annoyed, flushed, frazzled, I ran up the steps. Our doors were never locked, I grumbled to myself. Why must I be summoned to let in a customer? Flinging the door wide, not caring who heard me, I blurted out, "Welcome to Hell."

"So soon?" Gabriel Larue stood in the doorway. "No judgment first? Misinformed, was I?"

"*Sacre Bleu!*" The words slipped from me.

"In a bakery?" His gaze was attentive and, again, amused. "Who'd have thought it?"

"I *never* say that out loud."

"I do, from time to time."

"I spoke better in the dark." I ran a hand across my damp face. My hair, so red, so riotously curly, was unraveling from its knot atop my head. I felt breathless and awkward and thrilled. "No doubt I looked far better, too."

"I like you with flour on your nose."

To make this moment even worse, I sneezed.

"Come in, come in," I said. "It's just that I'm not used to looking at you while we speak. I'll learn. But I didn't have to do both in the ruins."

"That *was* you up there."

His eyes were serious now. I could see the small squint lines at their corners. His face and hands were tanned from working out of doors. Again, he had the demeanor of a man and not a boy.

"I thought so," he said. "All those nights you walked with me in the ruins. Three weeks of nights. Three changes of the moon."

"Yes. I knew your voice the instant I heard it at the banquet." In seconds, I regretted this admission. When would I learn to hold my tongue? But he was smiling at me now. There seemed millions of unspoken words and hopes and thoughts hanging in the air between us.

"Last night." He smiled now. "Last night, when you appeared—I was a bit stunned. More than 'a bit.' Where were you before?"

"Near enough, just hidden away." I tried to make light of this. "You know us serving wenches, how we spy. I was upstairs in a storeroom, listening at cracks in the floor. I heard your voice and then I saw you for the first time—through a knothole. The banquet didn't look so pleasant."

"Bad one. Hated those things. The fighting. Those questions. You see why I prefer your company. The dark. The two of us. The ruins."

"I've missed them."

"Hoping, I went back."

"I panicked, I guess, that last night."

"Well. A girl alone. Trusting a stranger."

"But you weren't," I said. "Not really."

"Nor you. Cecile, I must tell you...."

"What is it?" I was watching him.

"I feel now as I did then. But...you?"

I nodded, suddenly too shy to speak. The silence warmed and flowed between us. I still could not believe the nearness of him in my world, my workspace. Still, the voice from the ruins went with this tall man, worldly, wry, strong, serious, amused.

"Those nights," I said. "I didn't know you were that glass-maker I saw in the forest. And now, considered for a great commission."

"Would it have mattered to you?"

I countered with my own question: "If you'd known I was only a baker? Would that have mattered? Does it now?"

"You're not 'only' anything, Cecile. If you promise not to run away from me this time, I must add—"

I braced myself. This day had cracked wide open, hatching as I'd not expected any day to do. I didn't want it all spoiled now. At last he spoke.

"In the ruins. I knew who *you* were."

He stopped, waiting to see if I would bolt but for some reason, I was no longer afraid. Nor was I totally surprised he'd found me out.

"I should have guessed," I started to laugh. "You're an artist and you see so much, so fast."

"Three nights. Your silhouette. Your walk. Your bearing. That gorgeous tangle of hair." He smiled. "I couldn't tell you."

"But why?" I was not accusing him now.

"To you, it *would* have mattered."

He was right, of course. If I had not felt invisible, unrecognized, I never would have talked to him at all. And now he stood before me, real and solid, no shadow, no silhouette.

No longer could he be a stranger or a magician in the forest. I didn't even know why he was standing in our shop, I realized. Before I could ask, I heard heavy steps on the cellar stairs. My stepfather was stomping toward us.

I didn't want to tell Gabriel that this man, when he was drunk, beat me for trifling mistakes or for no reason at all. Nor did I say how I would suffer if there was one slip, one hint, one word about those three weeks of wandering in the cathedral's ruins.

Perhaps I was thinking, guessing, hoping much too far ahead. But if I happened to be caught too near Gabriel Larue, there would be hell to pay for both of us. What seemed to be good fortune no longer appeared quite so simple. Now there was temptation paired with terror.

"Welcome to Hell," I said again.

"Not Heaven?" He smiled.

"Closer to Purgatory."

"*Sacre Bleu,*" Gabriel sighed.

~~~

"Welcome, welcome, a thousand and one welcomes." My stepfather bounded toward us. His voice was honeyed—then sharp as pepper.

"Louis! Gaston!"

Henri Dufort bellowed for his two apprentices and glowed with self-importance; even the tip of his nose seemed lit. "Finish downstairs—Gaston, mind the counter, we have an honored guest, the Master Glazier, soon to be, that is." He coughed and bowed to Gabriel. "What may *I* provide you, Sir?"

"Three things..." Gabriel hesitated. "I need your daughter and a bed." There was an awkward silence. "Not together," he added. "Not at once."

Nervous laughter rose from us all.

"But of course." My stepfather would go to any length to please. "That would be two things, sir. And the third would be—"

"Ah." Gabriel steadied his gaze. "Long tables with raised edges. You spread your dough on them. Good for my work, too."

The baker paused to make sense of this.

"Of course," my stepfather finally spoke. His voice sounded somewhat like a wheeze, squeezed from reluctant bellows. He would sooner hold tight to his tables than to me, but he would get something out of this, I knew. "You will need bread for your men, your workers, yes?"

"In time. Work space first. Long tables make fine drawing boards." Gabriel glanced my way. "And I'll need an assistant."

"You do my house too much honor, sir." My stepfather spoke as if he had just tasted expensive wine. The thought of new cathedral windows, designed in our bakery was almost too marvelous for him. "Allow me, sir, to show you everything, I trust we will serve you well and...."

Down the cellar steps they went while I thought about Gabriel's first requests. Someone had decided to lodge him in town where he could be observed. Leaning back against the wall, I tried to believe this was happening.

I soon learned the truth: it was vanity, not virtue, that brought Gabriel to our house. My stepfather, I soon discovered, had expected that morning's visit. A fine dissembler, he was, with an eye to the main chance.

He had already offered a spare bedchamber for Gabriel to the Bishop, as well all needed services. Our long tables, too, were part of the bargain. If asked, my stepfather would gladly give his virgin daughter to anyone.

In a way, he had.

The arrangement was settled in moments. Assistant glass-makers would go on working in the woods, as needed, with their own tools and ovens. Meanwhile their master would make his designs in our house. Twice a week he would take these out to his men for rendering.

In the end, the designs would lead to sample panels of stained glass to be judged by the Bishop, the School, the Chapter, and other clerics. Not to mention influential donors like Morrisot, perhaps the Count himself, I suspected.

Important work would be done here and Nicolette, smiling now, wanted Gabriel to note her own importance. As she ran our household, I knew, she pretended it was hers. I didn't care, I didn't mind. Let her have her masquerade. At least I wouldn't have to cook two meals a day for a few weeks.

"All is to your liking sir?" Now she dimpled prettily at the Master Glazier, on her own terrain.

He nodded but he looked at me.

Nicolette began to pout, her dark eyes narrowing, and she flounced out, with one last backward glance at Gabriel Larue.

I watched her go and immediately forgot her. There were greater mysteries to contemplate than the shifting moods of Nicolette. One surpassing mystery amazed me above others: How could humble settings stand unseen behind great works of art? And I did feel humble as I showed Gabriel my place of work: such a plain room for a would-be artist, once occupied by Henri's late partner. Still, it was a goodly size, two tables, tools and my pots of glazes.

Before my "dark friend," as I still thought him, I set out a feast of color, pouring each one into a bowl: reds from roses steeped in beet juice; yellows from mushrooms and certain mustards; blues from berries; purples from plums's skins; eggshells and bonemeal for white; precious saffron. And my all-purpose medium: honey.

Gabriel examined every hue, spreading them on small squares of glass he drew from his satchel. With his finger, he would smear a sweep of color on the glass, then hold it up before an oil lamp I had lit.

I offered him a wooden spoon. I had meant the spoon to help him smear the colors on the glass. He thought otherwise. Into a pot of strawberry glaze he dipped the spoon and then, his eyes on me, he lifted it, still level, to his lips. Slowly, he did what I had always longed to do.

He tasted red.

And then he passed the spoon to me. Our fingers brushed. I tasted the red from the spoon's bowl, still moist from his lips. Next we sampled blue. The spoon moved back and forth between us with sensuous swings and longer licks.

Our hands were stained with colors but we did not notice until later, when time began again. We tried yellowgold and mixed it with blue—and we savored each other's salty wetness as the spoon skimmed the air. Before we left the room, Gabriel dipped the spoon into one last pot.

He fed me green directly from his tongue.

■

N ever shortchange glory.
So I was taught and so I believe. When I heard Jean Morrisot's steel-gray voice upstairs in our house, I paid it no mind. I did not even wonder why the man was there. Had I known, I would have lost a morning that was glorious indeed.

Gabriel and I were off into the day, still colored by the last of a red sunrise. Once more we were together without others; once more we were in an enchanted place. This time it was a meadow, glimmering with wild flowers: firey oranges, golds like cats' eyes, the purples of dusk.

But not the right blue.

We looked for it in smoke.

We looked for in it fruit.

We looked for it in streams.

And all the while we watched for blue, obsessed with blue, we watched each other, sidewise, as we waded out into the grasses again. As he had done before, Gabriel took my hand.

"To be safe," he told me.

"Of course," I answered.

"Can't be too careful."

"Of course not."

What a morning had opened out around us. The light turned ordinary land into a living thing: La Beauce, surrounding Chartres, with vast, rich spreading cornfields. There the clouds left changing shadows like great hand prints and the crops rose, tall and tawny, just to brush us.

The sun made the grasses flame: entire fields on fire with such fierce beauty, it was not quite of this world—nor were we, wading through the tides that swept over grasses, faces, hair.

But I would lie to you if I said that day, and others like it, were all artistic efforts. Our conversing never stopped. And our converse, I must add, was not always poetic. It was woven of the stuff that passes between people who know each other well. But we always circled back to blue.

"Must find it," he said. "Fast."

"Fast?" I looked at him. "The cathedral's walls won't be in place for years."

"The Papal Legate: Here for one month." He stopped to think. "Six weeks at best."

"And he wants a sample in that time?"

"That blue. That 'gaze' he wants."

"How can he expect that of you?"

"To him Chartres matters a great deal. Sacred, yes. Holy, yes. And—I shouldn't say this."

"You can say it to me."

"Chartres Cathedral brought pilgrims. Thousands of them. Pilgrims bring revenue." He shook his head. "Beauty brings fame. And more pilgrims. Churchmen must consider that. I know they do."

"Maybe the Church wants a miracle."

"In the form of windows. Stained glass to stir the soul, stun Europe; draw more pilgrims. And a gifted Master Glazier. For me, one powerful sponsor might have made this easier. Or a famous studio of glass-makers as my own."

"Your men are the best, aren't they?"

"Hand-selected. Careful choices. But these men are not well-known. Not yet. Didn't want to use my father's workers. Didn't want to use his friends' names. Win or lose, I'll do this on my own."

"You've been about this art for years. Even as a child, you told me: School in winter, glass-work every summer." I was staunch in his defense. "You're known. And who else can make *and* paint glass? Why must you prove yourself?"

"This commission..." The muscles tightened in his jaw. "Everyone wants it. The prize of a lifetime."

"So it is. And you are more than equal to it. Your judges will see your windows in the Bishop's private chapel. I did, many times. They are *non pareil*, unequaled."

"*Merci,* Cecile." Gabriel kissed my hand. "That means more than you know. You see the way an artist does."

"*Merci a toi.*" I could hardly speak.

Gabriel's face relaxed and he smiled. We tramped in easy silence beside the River Eure, crossing its humpbacked bridges and ducking under ancient weeping-willow trees. They leaned toward the river like girls on their hands and knees, drying their long wet hair; I had knelt there myself, doing just that, I told Gabriel.

I tried to think of trees but my mind kept returning to this man beside me. Now I understood why he had escaped to the ruins all those nights. In his father's wake, he did indeed have much to prove. And time was short indeed.

We must find that blue for Gabriel's designs. If only I could pull it from the river or the air itself. If only this blue were a note of music I could sing—one of my other paltry gifts: a good thing, since my aunt and I were named for music's patron saint.

"How can I help?" I asked him.

"You do that now, Cecile."

He stopped and reached up through the willow trees bordering the river. Gabriel's long fingers brought down a bird's nest filled with small fragments of hatched blue eggs. I looked at them. I held my breath. He frowned. Still not right; not the color he was seeing in his mind.

He saw things differently from others, making new this river I had known all my life. The outline of light around a tree took human for him. He saw weeds and tall grass as plumes, as smoke, as quills—as simple shapes, alone. When he spoke of these, I saw them that way, too, and this seemed to please him as he led my eye.

"Where do colors glow?" I wondered aloud.

"Outside. Or in your aunt's bottles."

"And you find them everywhere," I said.

"That narrows it down." His voice again was wry and he began to laugh. "And me. A strange shy child, straining after colors, you must think. Never scrapping with the other boys—but I did after school. Fought, scuffled, ran. Went along with them to the Paris brothels."

"Often?" I did not like hearing this.

"Seldom, I confess, and a very long time ago. I was only fourteen. 'The monk,' they call me, among my artisans." He studied the sky. "I wait for what I want, like this blue."

While he talked, he still took my hand to lead me through knee-high grass or to step across a fallen log, there seemed nothing bold or bad about it. Not that anyone could see us.

But what would my stepfather say? The Bishop? Henri Dufort had mistresses and the Bishop had mercy. Few folk, if any, followed all the rules of conduct to perfection. The great architect Bonnet had a different kind of reputation.

Even Morrisot, the Bishop's brother had dalliances before his marriage. Nicolette knew all the details. She knew of priests who strayed. We were doing nothing wrong. I put such thoughts from my mind and let myself delight in my companion.

When the sky changed and the rain came, it startled us. Together, we occupied a charmed place from some life, some time, where there could be no rain. When we finally agreed that it was real, we looked at the rain and said, in one voice: "*Blue.*"

But not the right blue.

Soaked, we ran back to Gabriel's forest shed, which he would shortly leave. It seemed a shame, for he had made perhaps five dozen glass fragments in varied shades of blue. These he had hung from strings nailed up all over the ceiling of the shed.

I laughed aloud, listening to the glass chips click against themselves like icy twigs and throw their flashing blues around the simple room. The shed was a like a wizard's cave—until I started shivering. My soaked clothes had gone cold.

Gabriel fetched his cloak, wrapped me in it and wrapped his arms around the cloak. I will never know how many moments I stood there, enfolded in his warmth. It could not have been so very long; it could not be long enough.

"Time for me to get back," I had to say.

How I dreaded what would happen then.

■

I expected to be beaten for staying out so long. My stepfather, however, was in an oddly generous and genial mood when I returned home. The high story of our house, jutting out over the narrow street, revealed to me the old fox watching from an upstairs window.

He was in the solar, as we called it: the sitting room and my stepfather's bedchamber. It lay above what Henri Dufort dared to call the "The Great Hall" and the entry stairs. Listening, I climbed those stairs and found my stepfather perched there on the longest bench, where he looked expectant—almost glad to see me.

That was the first strange thing. The next one was the solar itself. The room looked too clean, too polished, its stools and benches neatly rearranged, its cupboard newly scoured.

A fistful of ivy filled the blue pitcher on an open table where I always set wild flowers. Oil lamps were lit: a rarity by day. The expensive feather mattress, my inheritance, was displayed on its rope slats, and spread with my best tablecloth.

Something odd was happening—or was about to occur. My stepfather was keen to show off his property, it seemed.

But why?

"Well, my girl," the baker wheezed. "You're about to have a special caller. You. Imagine that."

There was a certain smugness in his tone that worried me: his business voice, the voice he used to seal a deal, or worse, settle an account. What was he about? Had he tinkered with my life somehow?

Now I heard slow footsteps on the stairs. My stepfather showed his guest up to the solar and offered him a seat by our shuttered windows. I looked into the flinty eyes of Jean Morrisot. Why did I always feel chilled by this man?

I had heard enough about him to stir some sympathy: the death of his only son, the loss of his wife, his loneliness despite his great success in commerce. His love of art. His refusal to give in to age and, sometimes, illness. As he entered the house and looked at me, his dark eyes were paired inkwells, catching some small spill of light.

"M'amselle, Cecile," he inclined his head.

"M'sieur Morrisot." I bobbed a curtsy.

"I trust you find the weather fair."

"Indeed, sir, I do."

"Warm for July."

"Indeed it is, sir."

A long taut silence.

Now, I lowered my eyes and waited, feeling an odd rush of fear. This man would not be here unless he wanted something from us. *Gets what he wants, that one,* Nicolette had said. I recalled how Morrisot had studied me the night before, at the Bishop's feast.

"I won't waste your time." His voice and eyes sharpened. "Cecile, I came this morning to ask your stepfather for your hand. I came back now to tell you this myself."

"My hand." I stalled. "You asked for—"

"Marriage, girl," my stepfather hissed.

"And your stepfather said he was agreed."

"Agreed?" I sounded like a dolt, I knew. I wanted to. Wealthy gentlemen do not tend to marry dolts. Especially dolts new to prosperity. I wished I could open the shutters and fly out the window.

"You stand amazed, girl, show your manners." The baker, my betrayer, scolded me and clicked his tongue twice in reproof.

"This appears sudden to you?" Morrisot's voice was curt. "Answer honestly."

"Yes, sir." I looked up at him.

"I have watched you often, M'amselle."

I said nothing. Outside, I heard children laughing in the street; they seemed very far away. Sunlight splashed across the floor, just before my feet, but it seemed distant, too. The morning's glory must have been only my imaginings.

"An odd match, you think it?" Morrisot's eyes flicked, knife-like, over me. "Here I am, your senior by more than three decades." His tone was formal, factual and dry. "I am of a higher social station, a different rank in life."

"Indeed you are, sir," I said.

He did not smile as he went on.

"My brother, His Excellency, finds this match unsuitable and he opposes it." For a moment, Morrisot studied the sleeves of his green silk tunic.

I could breathe again. "Of course, unsuitable, to say the least. I can't imagine why you—"

Morrisot raised a hand to cut me off. "As I told my brother, I *will* arrange a new life for myself. It may take some time." How calculated was his every word. "I have all a man could want, but for these: a lasting memorial, a son, and a wife."

"Sir, I would not do at all."

"You are too bold. But a beauty."

"Sir, I am not." I let myself sound brazen. "There are many other girls—"

"You contradict me?" He squinted.

I looked at him. "I speak true."

"Another contradiction from you."

"A habit to dislike in me, I'm sure."

"On the contrary." He offered a thin smile. "I admire spirit. And you have good stock, I think, in your maternal line."

"My aunt is only an apothecary. And in strain-ed circumstances," I added. "Her mother was gentry, but that was long ago."

"A wealthy match would be of great benefit to her. You might consider your duty to her and to your stepfather when you flinch from me." His voice was sharp. "I must seem harsh."

"You do, sir." I wanted to sound bolder still.

"Shut it, girl," my stepfather hissed.

There was a long and awkward pause which seemed to frost the sun filled room. I kept my eyes fixed on Morrisot and prayed he would leave.

"Cecile," my stepfather hissed again. "Out of every girl in Chartres, he has chosen...*you*."

The baker was thrilled, of course, at the prospect of such a match. He now looked like a man contemplating a rich and satisfying meal.

"If His Excellency objects—" I began.

"Is this such a dreadful fate?" Morrisot gave me his wintry smile but his eyes turned hard. "Is there someone else?"

"There is," I blurted out. "Indeed, yes."

"A marriage contract?" Morrisot pressed.

"Awaited." I took a breath. "Expected."

"I told you to shut your mouth, girl." The baker grabbed my arm. "There is no contract in the offing, my lord, I assure you. Pay Cecile no mind."

"Nor will there be a contract between us unless I can change the Bishop's views." Morrisot's eyes narrowed once more. "This may be difficult."

"You will try, sir?" I asked.

"I will fund a wall of windows in the new cathedral—under two conditions." Morrisot spoke at last. "The windows must meet my expectations. The bride must be my choice." He tapped a bowl of grapes with a finger. To me, the sound was like a tolling bell.

"Surely, there are more suitable brides." On purpose, I spoke out of turn. "Our Nicolette, of your own class, now she is a true beauty." I could see her peeking through the door, just cracked. "She knows your world, I do not."

"You are quite outrageous, my girl." Jean Morrisot stared at me. "And outspoken."

"Yes." I wanted to sound as flawed as possible.

"I rather like daring in a woman. But I must ask who is this 'other' contender for your hand?"

"I cannot say, my lord."

"Cannot? Will not?" Morrisot moved toward me and I saw anger in his eyes. "Which?"

"Will not," I stood firm.

"You don't know me, Cecile." He lowered his voice. "You know nothing of my loneliness. You know nothing of my passion for beauty. I yearn for a rare beauty in our cathedral's windows—this I must somehow ignite."

"No doubt you will do that."

"I also seek beauty in a wife. Think on this, Cecile. I'll not force you." He looked hard at me again. "Not yet, I think. Not yet."

"I'll be sure she thinks on this." My stepfather's voice was ominous and oily. "She has no right to question you or any of the honors heaped on us this day. Your proposal first, of course. And the young glass-master seeking a bed here."

"I see." Morrisot's gaze deepened and something in it changed. "Your stepfather tells me that you were out this morning with M'sieur Larue."

This was not a question. "And you found his company to your liking?"

"He is a congenial man." I tried for caution.

"And he found you so, as well." Morrisot's canny eyes appeared to light. "Surprising: the cold-natured artist, alien to love and passion. Even the passion to create glorious glass...or so I hear. 'Congenial,' you call him. And you flush."

"Polite," I added quickly. "Polite, that's what I meant to say. I'm nervous near you, sir. Polite."

"Interesting." The frosty man still watched my face. "Most interesting. All this shall work to my purpose. I have found our meeting quite instructive. You tremble, Cecile?"

"No sir. Did you think I should?"

"You answer questions with questions?"

"Do I, sir?"

"You see. Impertinence. I'll beat that girl." My stepfather was already reaching for his belt and I was already moving away. I knew what would happen to me after Morrisot was gone.

"I wouldn't do too much of that, Dufort." Morrisot frowned. "Whoever weds her will not want to see her scarred."

Morrisot nodded at us and went out into the day. Now I would get my beating and he knew it and he did not stay to stop it. An impertinent baker's daughter well deserved a beating, he must have thought, however light it was. He even tried to make light of it. That was a thing I could never forget, never quite forgive.

"Welcome to Hell," I whispered as my stepfather, red-faced, breathing hard, came at me with a knotted cord.

∎

F inding Hell on earth is easy.

        Anyone, even a child, can do it.

Finding the way out of Hell has always been more difficult. This is what I learned in the span of one summer's day and night. I can still hear the bakery door close quietly behind Morrisot.

And I can still hear the sound of the baker's belt as it ripped through the air. He must have kept the merchant's words in mind, though; I only had three blows, rather than five, leaving my backside bruised. I pressed my palms together and refused to cry out.

When the whipping was done, my stepfather stood back, sweating, his eyes tired and reddened. The day's excitement and exertion seemed to drain him; he retired early, his supper scarcely touched. Nicolette, exhausted from the laundering, likewise was early abed.

I doused the lamps and once the town had gone quite dark, I trudged to the cathedral ruins once more. Gabriel and I had decided this was still the safest place to meet at night. Even so it was a slow and painful walk for me up the steeper streets.

Moving through the back lanes of the terraced town, I remembered there were people who slept deeply, dreamlessly, and knew no dread of the next dawn, the coming day.

With each step, I could feel the welts left on my skin. I knew why I was doing this: if Gabriel was not there in the ruins, at least I would have a sense of nearness to him. That itself would be healing.

I winced as I neared La Rue au Lait. Then I saw the cathedral's towers flanking the remaining Western Wall between them, outlined for the first time this month by full moonlight.

Gabriel was there. I could make him out, as always, in front of the South Tower's door. Nothing stirred; no air, no snapping twig, no wandering cat. I winced again as I moved toward him.

"Cecile?" He frowned. "You're hurt?"

"The baker only hit me thrice."

"A beating? On my account?"

"No, no, on mine." I tried to make nothing of it. "My bold tongue, it always gets me into trouble."

I told him about Morrisot. Gabriel's face changed with each word, as if he pictured everything in segments, like the stories in a stained glass window, and in fact, I learned, he did.

"Here, this stone," he said. "Sit down."

"I can't. He hit me where I sit."

"That Henri," Gabriel's voice stung. "I'll have words with him tomorrow."

"Not the best way to begin." I had to smile.

"It won't be easy there. Beneath his roof."

"It's my roof, too." I touched Gabriel's cheek.

"Never have we been here under a full moon." He looked amazed, as if an autumn tree had bloomed and borne fruit. The light changed the ruins, silvering them with a touch of vanished splendor.

Most of the rubble had been cleared away and a great open space lay behind the West Wall and the two towers. If all went well, that space would soon be filled with workmen. I turned from the debris back to Gabriel.

"How did you know to come?"

"I hoped you might—" He looked down.

"I hoped, too." I took a long breath.

In the full moon's light, the cathedral's wall stood, shield-like and protective, as if its towers could stand watch for us. Beyond, the cruciform outlines of the old church spread wide, opening before us—a cathedral made of air as he had once described it.

We walked toward the nave's old center aisle, still visible in the sturdy old stone floor. The aisle had been worn down into a gentle groove; it had run through other cathedrals built here for over hundreds of years. I thought of all those pilgrims walking here; all those seekers, all those penitents. All those brides.

Without a word, Gabriel led me down the aisle. There we stood before the marks left by the altar. There we faced each other, my hands in his, as couples stand together when they wed.

"Love you, Cecile."

"As I love you," I whispered

A pause. "Marry me?"

"I want nothing more."

"Your stepfather—?"

"He may refuse," I said.

"Then let it be now."

"And here. On holy ground."

"The cathedral will preside."

For us, this was a reverent moment in God's presence. We knelt where countless couples had knelt before us and we spoke their words and bound each other with our vows; our pledges before God.

As we made those ancient promises, I heard them anew. Our words were good and graced, with a rightness all about them. This could be no sin, no sacrilege, I thought. This was simply true.

After our "Amens," Gabriel lifted me to my feet and kissed me—and in that sacred silence, I heard a stifled cough. We were not alone as we'd supposed; an intruder was somewhere behind us. As I turned, Gabriel turned.

Together, then, we saw him.

Crouched by the Royal Portal, Jean Morrisot was watching us as keenly as a hunter watches his prey. He did not try to hide from us. Moonlight caught the glimmer in his eyes before he slipped away into the dark.

~~~

Nothing changed.

Everything changed.

The day Gabriel came to live in our house, I felt our small world shifting. Rarely can a single day change a life but sometimes it does happens. It was so for us on an ordinary Tuesday morning.

That clear summer day, I saw long skeins of open time and space unreeling ahead. It was only the beginnings of things I saw then. The start of living and working with Gabriel. The start of sleeping under the same roof. The start of making our own home together.

It was also the start of trouble.

I did not see this on a day of sun and passing clouds and light melting like butter on the window sills. My stepfather was about the baking with his apprentices. Nicolette was scrubbing the kitchen floor. I was left to settle Gabriel in his new room.

"When he came into his money, my stepfather joined the two houses next door with this one," I explained. "He likes to show how...prosperous we are. That's how we got to have three bedchambers. Rare for most bakers, yes, but not Henri Dufort. In fact, he bought out another baker to expand our space."

Gabriel seemed to find charm in my speech. Again I saw amusement and tenderness in his level gray gaze. He carried two satchels and had a third strapped to his back; best to travel with few "encumbrances," he said, and I heartily agreed, though I had never traveled anywhere at all.

"And so this is our house, your house." My words ran together like a spill of hurried steps. "I'm glad, we're all glad you are come." *Dolt*, I chided myself silently. *Shut up, Cecile.* "We rarely have guests, I hardly know what words to speak."

"Of course." He ran a finger down my face. "Easier last night. Always. In the dark."

We both remembered that—as well as my punishment, yesterday as well; I still could not sit down. Gabriel asked me about my pain but I made light of it.

"What pain? It's gone, quite gone."

"Can't be. Brave girl. That stepfather of yours." He kept back his anger. "I'm glad of this space, even so. Better than the forest now."

I led him through the doubled house. Branching out from the next stair landing were the bed-chambers and above them, the attic space where Nicolette slept.

"This was mine, now it will be yours." I showed Gabriel into my bedchamber. "If it suits you." I began to realize how dangerous this plan could be. "Most of our chambers have doors," I added. "I expect my stepfather will lock me in at night." Was I joking? I didn't know, myself.

"You're giving up your room for me?" Gabriel looked up and shook his head. "Won't do, can't take your bed." Made of canvas, stuffed with wool, the bed rested on a frame strung with thick ropes, interlaced. All was topped another worn feather mattress: part of my stepfather's inheritance.

"It's all arranged, all planned, all settled, believe me." My words tumbled over themselves like someone falling down the stairs. "You'll be across from the boys' room, the apprentices. I'll be down the hall. I have a good bed for myself and that chamber is a comfortable space." In fact, it had been a storeroom but I didn't mention that.

"Sounds proper enough." Gabriel laughed.

"Even though propriety is hardly my stepfather's *forte*." I laughed as well.

We looked away from each other and then I saw the colored streaks I'd left on my bed chamber's window. Why had I not noticed them when I was readying the room? Or maybe I had hoped Gabriel would see them. Probably the latter, I thought. For the first time, he noticed my own artwork on glass.

"You painted here, Cecile?"

"With my own glazes. I've always painted." I never told him this before. "My mother was a glass-painter herself."

"Really?" He glanced at me. "Painting is hard. I know. This is good. Do more."

"If all's to rights, I'll fetch linens."

We exchanged a quick look across the bed. Finally Gabriel looked away and lifted a few of his things out of his satchels: charcoal sticks, a copybook, glass shards. I watched all these drawn out, one by one, to rest in his long-fingered hands.

Next, he held up a small stained glass image of a saint, the size of a biscuit: St. Lucy, I knew, was the patron saint of painters.

"Sad history she has, poor Lucy." Gabriel blew dust off the image in his palm. "Not a pretty one, her story, but it came right in the end."

"Tell me." I sat, unthinking, on the bed.

"Blinded, Lucy was, rather than give up her faith. But a miracle from God restored her sight. Now she helps others see more clearly."

"Ah. I'm glad she has her eyes here in your rendering." I watched him hang the saint in the window. "Does she go everywhere with you?"

"Everywhere. Since I was twelve. She was my mother's." His movements were so deft, so definite. "This was my mother's as well."

On a cord around his neck hung one ring: a plain and narrow band. "Goes with me, too."

"Your mother's?" I dared ask and he nodded. "I kept my mother's ring as you did. But I'm not clever enough to make a saint from colored glass."

"Painted on your wall, didn't you?," he reminded me. "We'll share St. Lucy."

The room, still and warm, leaned over us. The rafters were so low, he had to duck his head from time to time, as he hung his clothes from them, the way we all did then.

Already, somehow, this chamber seemed to be his own, ready for him to come and claim it. I had often thought how odd I'd feel in bed with a man. Now my thoughts were rather different.

Even so, I was flustered by Gabriel's nearness in this, my room, his room, our room. To hide my nervousness, I threw open the shutters with great energy and that was how the bird happened to fly in.

I gasped aloud and drew back from its flapping wings: a dove, come through the window, now confused and trapped. A whirlwind of white, this was no dove to stuff into a pie.

Some say it is good luck when a bird flies into a house; some say it is bad luck, foretelling an ending or an accident or a death. I say it is one damned nuisance, whatever its meaning. Feathers were already drifting down.

We stood watching the panicked dove dart and swoop and fly around the room, unable to find its way out. Finally it lighted on a rafter just above the center of the bed.

My stepfather would have beaten the creature with a broom. My mother would have seen it as a holy messenger. I decided to take her view. What would my aunt say about this winged intruder?

"Maybe it's a sign from the Holy Ghost," I suggested. "Or a sign to keep the shutters closed."

Gabriel was taking off his shoes. In a moment he was standing on the bed; there he kept his balance, crouching under the low ceiling.

Shoeless now, myself, showing just a bit of my black stockings, I climbed up beside him. The feather mattress kept shifting beneath our weight. Hushed, we wobbled there together for a moment.

And then, with one swoop, Gabriel had the dove in hand; the next moment he let the bird fly out the window. But that was not the end of it. Still standing on the bed, he took my hand. "For balance," he grinned. "Of course," I said.

"My heavens!" There was a cough at the threshold of the room. Nicolette was peering around the doorframe, her eyes wider.

"*Sacre Bleu.*" She had been watching us. "It sounded as if you were doing something else in here. Something I would never repeat." I could see the envy in her eyes. "Of course."

We all filed down both flights of stairs, while Nicolette smiled prettily at Gabriel. She kept turning her head to look at him behind her, and she swung her hips more than usual, I thought.

How she hoped he would be comfortable, she said. How she hoped he would enjoy his stay. How she hoped he would let her know his needs.

How I wished I could clap my hands over her ripe mouth, tinted with crushed raspberries.

I reminded myself that she flirted with the rich banker as well, and with certain merchants she had known before her father's business failed. From time to time, she even flirted with my stepfather.

And so I did not see the danger growing like a weed within her—no threat from Nicolette that simple sun-struck day.

■

A s a rule I don't trust luck.

It has a way of running out when things are going well. We were having a sweet streak of luck, I knew, and I hoped we might escape its ending for once. Certainly nothing could go wrong on a day of sacred celebration.

That next Sunday the people of Chartres gathered for the blessing of the cathedral's first stone. In this ceremony, the main role belonged to Jacques Bonnet, the new Master of Works, and Gabriel's ally in the "color wars." I liked this big mason and it pleased us all to watch him set in place the start of our new sanctuary.

Now, before the gathering, Bonnet labored to carry that heavy rock, with aid from his apprentices. But not enough aid. Not nearly enough, I was surprised to see. I noted the veins standing out in the master's neck and head. I could see how his color change as he sweated and strained.

Even so, Bonnet was a strong man, widely experienced, famous for his work. It was likely he had performed this task in the other churches he so brilliantly designed. It was only the heat. It was only nerves. Soon he would be to rights. He had to be.

The Mass began as always "*In Nomine Patris, et Fílii, et Spíritus Sancti.*"

"Amen." We crossed ourselves.

"*Dóminus vobíscum,*" the Bishop chanted.

"*Et cum spírito tuo,*" we replied.

I was standing toward the back of the throng with my aunt. Straight and tall and still beautiful, she made me proud. I was always by her side at Sunday Mass, where I could almost inhale her prayerful presence.

As ever, she smelled of herbs and autumn. Nearby, I glimpsed Gabriel—strange to watch him in this place that had, so recently, been our own terrain. He looked at me; I knew he was thinking much the way I was.

"*Kýrie eléison....*"

Mass was the holiest of times, but I must admit some looks were often exchanged throughout its duration. Nicolette kept turning around to gaze at Bonnet who stood behind us. His face remained flushed, almost purple. He was neither young nor old, but clearly, he was exhausted.

"*Christe eléison....*"

Behind us, we heard a gasp. Looking over my shoulder, I saw Bonnet jerk backwards, reeling and struggling for breath. Before I could speak, the big man staggered away from the crowd and stumbled toward the old cathedral's remaining West Wall.

I saw him leaning on the Royal Portal, throwing his massive weight against it. I told myself it was only the heat that had affected him. He was a proud man; he would not like a lot of fuss and flurry around him, of that we could be sure.

"*Kýrie eléison*," the Bishop chanted.

With my aunt, I watched Bonnet. This could not be happening, I thought. That man could not be taken ill, not here, not now. As if he could hear me somehow, he lurched to the North Tower, there staggered around it and beyond it, out of sight.

Bonnet's absence grew longer—too long. My aunt slipped away, following the mason now. When she did not reappear, Gabriel turned to follow them as well. Moments passed. The Mass continued. I hastened outside.

As I left, the Bishop seemed small and far away: his voice sounded as if it traveled over water. I looked back once, then moved ahead, followed by Nicolette. Father Pierre was moving past the cathedral's the tower now, a look of alarm on his broad and fleshy face.

The Master of Works lay in the open square in front of the cathedral's West Wall. All about him was a splash of morning light but he seemed to sprawl in his own darkness.

His full lips, usually ruddy and robust, had lost their color. His skin was pallid now; his forehead glistened with sweat. Watching Bonnet, most of us began to bless ourselves; some already wept.

The mason's broad chest was heaving; my aunt cradled his head. Beside her on the ground, she had set her bottle of aromatic salts. There was no longer any use for them, that was plain. Despite my aunt's many gifts, she could do nothing now.

With the Holy Oils, Father Pierre's thumb impressed the Sign of the Cross on Bonnet's forehead; then the priest moved to anoint mouth, hands, heart, and feet. The Last Rites were a part of life, we knew, but this time each word, each gesture cast a darkness on my spirit as never before.

Next we heard those prayers we all knew too well. The somber words hung on the warm air along with smell of grass and earth and life. I felt Gabriel's shoulder press mine as we drew nearer and for a moment, we leaned against each other.

The fallen man's hands had turned a startling white; their fingertips, a faint blue. Bonnet, with all his strength, was straining, it seemed, to drink the air. Another splash of sun fell across the big man; I still can hear the rasping of his breath. Bonnet threw his huge head back and his dark eyes widened, rolling like those of a wounded animal.

Then, jolting forward, he appeared to catch hold of a sudden thought. Clearly in pain, he managed to scan the growing crowd around him. Gasping, he tried to speak. Finally, his eyes fixed on Gabriel's taut face. Bonnet reached for his friend's right hand and, with will and effort, wheezed a few words to him:

"Sorry...leaving you...alone...to fight...."

I could see Gabriel's left hand move to cover the mason's. Then a sudden spasm shook that great sprawled body, head to foot, and Bonnet heaved out one lingering harsh breath. We waited but he drew in no more air. His eyes, still open, saw nothing more of us or of that place.

We knelt beside him, crossing ourselves once again as the priest prayed for the soul of Jacques Bonnet: *"Requiem aeternam dona eis Domine et lux perpetua luceat eis..."*

"Eternal rest..." The familiar words fell among us and after they were said, the priest covered Bonnet's face. We had lost a good man and a good Master of Works. Already we all had lost so much. This left us with another unexpected wound.

Even so, as the mason would have wished, the Mass went on behind us. The bread and wine were consecrated and elevated for all to see. The Sanctus bells were rung. And the new cathedral's first stone would stay where Jacques Bonnet had placed it, struck just then by morning sun.

~~~

Never bear a corpse across a planted field.

This, it is widely known, may blight the crop and cause a disturbance in the general harmony of the field's surroundings. Never walk under a ladder. Never begin anything on Fridays. Never set a hat down on a bed. Never perform work without praying first. Everyone understands these things, or so they did in my youth, and if not now, more's the pity.

There is wisdom in these ancient customs and reminders of how fragile life can be. Objects fall from ladders, as do people; hats get crushed and serious work fills one's entire world.

As to the corpse—this I cannot quite explain, but mind you, I have never seen the truth of this old custom fail. Once again, it was proven on the day of Jacques Bonnet's funeral procession.

A sad day it was.

An unlucky day as well.

A man fell off his trotting horse.

A black dog tumbled down a well.

And Gabriel almost lost his right hand.

The pain and blood were bad enough. This also looked to be a mighty setback for him and the work toward his commission. Not to mention a start on the cathedral's windows. In part, I think, I was at fault. I invited Gabriel come with me to market and there, of all places, hidden trouble waited.

If he had made a stained glass window of the market, it would have been colorful and bright, held together by a tent that covered rows of smaller stalls. These went up on open ground around the cathedral's ruins where the cries of vendors peppered the air: *Ripe grapes, Ox tongues, Fresh asparagus....*

At the butcher's stall, there was always the stench of raw meat, often dripping blood onto the ground, and at the fishmongers, ladies sometimes held bags of crushed lavender to their noses.

The fruit stalls were my delight, piled with gem-like berries at this time of year: raspberries, blueberries, strawberries; green and red and purple grapes. Such richness of colors, such a variety of shapes, from wheels of cheese to hazelnuts.

Gabriel watched everything and everyone. His eyes narrowed as they moved from stall to stall, as if to memorize the pictures they made. It was as if he could see inside a pear, a pork chop and know the colors hidden there.

He smiled at me across a heap of chard and spinach. As I made my purchases, he carried them in a long mesh bag, slung over his shoulder. We spoke of food and flavors; we argued about mint.

And all the while, we watched each other from the corners of our eyes, discreet as ever in public. Still we were rubbing elbows, brushing shoulders, there in the light, in the real world. The only person watching us was a small and agile monk, but whenever I turned toward him he dodged away and managed to disappear.

"Come away with me," Gabriel whispered into my hair. "We'll set up housekeeping together."

"You're mad," I laughed but wished it so.

"Madness? Happiness, I call it."

"A few more things, then home."

Pushing through the crowd of hagglers and hawkers, we glimpsed that monk again, an old gnarled toad of a man. Every time we turned, he spun about and hid his face inside his cowl. A moment later he was somewhere else, always squinting at us.

"Friend of yours?" Gabriel's voice was dry.

"Never saw the man before." I shuddered.

"I have." He frowned. "But where?"

"Never mind him then, here, taste."

I held up a ripe pear and we both bit into it at once, he on one part of the curve, I at the other, and the juice ran down our chins. We laughed and wiped each other's faces; our lips came close to meeting at the fruit's thinning core. That morning, Gabriel told me, numbered among the best of his life.

Until, of course, luck twitched its fickle tail.

Yet again, I felt someone's eyes on us and, looking up, I saw the monk slip behind the knife-grinder's stall. The whetstone was at rest for the moment and Gabriel went to buy a sharp knife with a good blade for shaving.

The little knife-grinder sat grinning by his wheel. He always grinned in that elfin way and like a sprite he looked, sharpening any tool to a fine edge, while hot blue sparks flew about him.

This was a tented stall with a mesh backing, where there hung a wide variety of knives—his glinting metal wares caught the sun. Gabriel studied them; his long lean frame seemed taller still beside the little knife-grinder, with a gap-toothed grin.

I saw one quick movement: a monk's black robe behind the mesh. And then it came: that crash I still can hear. From the back, someone had overturned the stall, shoving it forward at an angle.

Dozens of bright knives were pointing outward as the stall came down. To my horror, some of the blades grazed Gabriel. Though he managed to dodge the largest share of it, while the nimble knife-grinder escaped entirely.

Behind the stall, I saw the monk spring away but little did I care for him just then: Gabriel stood there, bleeding. For a moment he looked stunned; then with a burst of fury, he pushed the stall back. Blood streamed from his right hand; blood ran down his upraised arm.

"Oh God oh God oh God," the knife-grinder kept chanting as I pushed my way through the gathering crowd. "Oh holy Jesus God."

When I reached Gabriel, he managed a strained smile. "You should see your face," he winced.

"How bad is it?" My voice shook.

"One hand. I think. A scratch."

It was more than just a scratch, I knew, but all the same, Gabriel was fairly fortunate; those knives could have stabbed his body in a dozen places. He had moved just fast enough, shielding himself with his right hand—his drawing hand, his working hand.

In my distress for Gabriel, I did no chase that devious wily monk who, in any case, darted away.

■

When she saw me with a bloodied man, my aunt threw down her sewing and leapt to her feet.

She hastened to the entrance of her apothecary shop and threw wide the door, causing its small string of bells to chime. I looked shaken and white, I know, because she gave me a tonic of some kind. I drank it while she examined the slash across Gabriel's right hand.

Thank God for her, I thought. As I have noted, this woman was more than an ordinary relative to me; she was a second mother. It was she who had kept my childhood knit together in one long strong skein. Her gaze was steady as a candle flame in a still room and that room always smelled of nutmeg and dried roses and vanilla.

She was wise; famous for it. Tall and slender, this woman-tree, her arms branching out to us as shelter. At thirty-six, she appeared to have no age.

Her brown eyes, like butternuts, were warm but sharp; her fingers were deft with those needing physic of all kinds. No one else could attend Gabriel better.

Now my aunt moved his fingers, one by one, and swabbed the gash with cider vinegar. Gabriel winced once more but let no sound escape him. As my aunt probed the wound, I had to look away. When she finished, I dreaded what she would say. It was her custom to be honest in all things, even if she had to give bad news.

"Not too deep, nothing severed that can't heal." She looked up. "In time."

"Thank God." I crossed myself.

"*In time,*" she repeated. "*With rest.*"

"Time?" Gabriel frowned. "How much?"

"Ah, you men," my aunt sighed.

I had to laugh as we thanked her.

Now my aunt's words were tonic enough for me, even though I knew that there would be some pain before the healing. I found myself unable to watch her work with the gash, drawing folds of skin together, forcing them to meet.

Feeling queasy, I glanced around this familiar shop. It felt like my real home. Here my mother's parents had lived and worked and here I had passed much of my earliest years.

Here, too, I was quietly instructed about female "unmentionables," like the start of my monthly bleeding at the age of twelve. That event became unexceptional and expected; different in every way different from the blood before me now.

Now I saw how shabby the place had grown; my aunt's fortunes had declined. All was scrubbed and clean but the furniture looked weary; the few cushions were threadbare, balding, and mended. My mind flashed to Morrisot's words about my duty. Would my aunt like to think of herself as "a duty?" I booted that thought away, as if I could kick it down the stairs.

"Yes, you'll do," my aunt was telling Gabriel. "Even so, you must *not* use your hand for a few days. You understand me, yes?"

"What would be 'a few?' " He persisted.

"One week. Absolutely *no drawing.*"

Across the gash, she spread a fresh spider's web: a fine gauze to help the wound mend. Before Gabriel could stand up, she applied clove oil to numb the pain and then an herbal poultice. Finally she wrapped the hand with a cloth bandage.

"Too much fuss, too much bother for you, Madame—" he began. "But I'm grateful."

"No bother at all, Cecile wants this for you."

"Still too much—" The common growls of an injured man. "I'll do. Sooner than you think."

"Indeed? We shall see, won't we?"

My aunt and I exchanged a smile. She had the kind that smooths the air in any room. Some said she had the gift of Second Sight but this was never mentioned in her house.

These days, it was far too easy for someone, anyone to cry, "Witch" against her and find believers. This was a potent danger for widows with property. I cast such thoughts away from me.

"Cecile tells me you search for a new shade of blue?" My aunt was asking Gabriel.

"Searching," he said. "Not finding."

"You need not search too far, I think."

"Madame, how can I thank you?"

"Heal." She refused the coins he offered.

I slipped a few onto the counter when my aunt did not see. Her money troubles were never discussed and she would accept no charity. Instead she'd begun to take in some sewing; a younger apothecary had begun to take in some of her customers.

If I married well, my stepfather would often say, that would take good care of her. In a flash I thought of Morrisot's proposal; then I turned back to Gabriel. My aunt caught the look I gave him and the one he returned to me.

"You mean a great deal to our Cecile," she told him with certainty—and courtesy as well.

"And she to me. Past telling."

"Some gifts are brief but deep enough for life." she looked away. "But let us not think too far ahead, only of your hand, sir. A hand *at rest.*"

My aunt filled her wooden cups with ale.

As she did, I saw the stretcher, or litter, leaning on one wall: canvas stretched across two long wooden poles. My aunt made these up to serve the ill and the dead. I'd heard that she had made the litter for Bonnet. And then I turned my mind to laughter, ale, and healing.

~~~

Later, at home, we found Gabriel's hand was bandaged far too artfully for him to use. Should the Bishop's assistant be informed? No sketches of the windows could be made for days.

Not only would work be delayed. Now there was an enemy who crept about outside and might creep near again. I did not even know his name—that strange and devious brother vowed to the monastery of Abbot Chevan.

Was the monk acting for this abbot, so opposed to "still more colored glass" in the new cathedral? Was this a secret and private mission? One thing the Brother had was zeal, to be sure. Less sure was where we'd seen this creature before.

"I remember him now." I thought back. "At the Bishop's banquet. Yes. The palace."

"The monk was there? You saw him?"

"With Abbot Chevan." I was certain.

"Chevan's not a madman, is he?"

"No." I paused. "The monk might be."

When I poured more ale, Gabriel saw that my own hand was trembling. "Cecile. I'll mend. It's over."

"Not quite." I sighed. "Not quite yet."

How to put into words the way this wounding made me feel? It was as if I myself had done the bleeding. If only I could; my hands were not so valuable and could be spared.

"Have to work," he said at last.

"My aunt told me to calm you."

"Lock me up? Take away my charcoal?"

"No joking. That's your drawing hand."

"I know, I know. But time is short and there is so much to do." I could feel the tension in his body and his need to move, to act, to start his sketches and designs. No window could come without a design: first in miniature, then a larger pattern, pane-by-pane.

Gabriel looked ahead to years of work; each window would hold many panels, many sectioned stories from the Bible. Likely he looked back on his father's work, too. So often it was held up before him. Well I knew how Gabriel felt the press of time to prove himself and now that time was tight.

"What are you thinking of?" I asked.

"Designs. More pictures to come."

"That's not enough for you, is it?"

"Ah. Found out." He kissed me.

"I know you have older designs."

"Not enough. New ideas burst in."

"Then let you go and look at things you would put in your windows. Let you plan and plot and scheme in that whirling mind of yours, I know it's never still." I tried to sound maternal, firm, stern. "But do *not* draw. Agreed?"

We gazed around the solar as if it held a way to save his hand and the week's lost work. From the street there rose the sounds of working folk: Voices calling in the street and a workman whistling. Carts and footsteps passed below us. I knew I would never keep him in the house.

"So many windows waiting. Some with thirty panels each. Some, I hear, twenty-five feet tall." He began to think out loud. "Stories. Saints. The Bible, from Creation on...."

He paused, searching his mind.

"What else? There's more. Common folk. Never see them pictured in cathedral windows."

"Saints and prophets, noblemen at prayer, that's what I've noticed." I had never stopped to wonder about this. It had always been so.

"Not right, is it?" I saw how tight his jaw was set. "Workers should stand by saints."

"Yes." I watched the light haloing his face. "I'm sure the clergy wants that—donations from each trade's confraternity. Their figures will 'sign' each given window. That's my best guess."

"Figures drawn from life?"

" 'Stock poses,' most likely."

"From the Glass-makers' Copybook?"

"You're disappointed," I sighed.

"Repeat my father's figures?"

"You'll make them your own."

"How?" Gabriel's voice cut.

"Paint. Faces, hands, folds, hair—"

"Not enough." His face was tight.

"It may have to be," I told him.

"Don't fight me on this, Cecile."

"I'm afraid for you." I flared up.

"My work, done *my* way."

"What about using *two* ways?"

"Of all people, Cecile... *you* can't understand. You can't see art, just politics. Thought you could."

His words seared my soul. I made no reply. Hurt and angry, I didn't try to find a way to untangle all these threads. For a while, we sat together in a hot tight box of silence. I didn't move or look at Gabriel.

Finally, his hands closed over mine.

"Didn't mean that," he whispered.

There was a long strained pause.

"I know." My voice was reedy, thin.

"What I said...it wasn't true."

Another pause like stretched string.

"Hurt you, my Cecile. Sorry for it."

A longer pause, a fretful one.

"I know," I said, stronger then.

"Forgive me? A stubborn man?"

"Yes."I touched his face. "And yes."

The weather in our house had changed as if a wind had shifted, but there was still one question to be answered. I had tried to avoid it after seeing Gabriel's bandage. Now I took a breath and put words to my fear.

"How will you set down your ideas?"

A silence drained air from the room.

"Draw for me? Only a week?"

I stared at Gabriel. "I can't."

"You paint. Sculpt. Sketch. Yes?"

He was already halfway up the stairs to get his things: his drawing boards, his sticks of charcoal, his tools. His chalked boards were prepared. But I was not. This time, I was certain, I would fail him.

~~~

"Cecile. Steady your hands."

"I told you—I can't do this."

"You can, my clever girl."

"Flattery gets you...anywhere."

We practiced with the charcoal first, I am ashamed to say, on my small room's wall. I liked the feel of those black sooty sticks between my thumb and forefinger. I even liked the way they smelled.

Still, I liked much less the way my fingers sketched what I saw: a bench, a pitcher, the chest. I was out of practice. Also, I was used to painting more decorative subjects; my specialty was flowers.

These early attempts were embarrassments to me. It wouldn't do, this dismal experiment, no matter how fine its sound. I wanted to give up but I knew Gabriel would be disappointed.

He guided, encouraged, corrected, praised. With me, he managed to be patient. Outside, I drew with a stick in the moist ground. My arm tired, my hand ached, but soon I had surprised myself. As I went on my shapes came clearer, true and sharp.

"Draw your shoes," Gabriel directed.

"My shoes?" I stared at him.

"Go on, Cecile, you can."

The strange thing was: I could, I did.

"Loosening your wrist, your arm," he urged me. "There. Good. Better. Quick strokes. Don't think too much. Look up. Look out. Yes. Draw that tree."

I tried. Under my hand a tree began to take shape. The charcoal seemed to move all on its own, though I must admit, I had drawn trees before with my homemade glazes. At one time, in raspberry sauce, I had smeared a forest on my wall. Sketching what he next asked was harder:

"Catch that woman. In the road."

I was never happy with figures I'd drawn. Even so, I reached for what I knew and kept my eyes, as he instructed, on the woman I was drawing. At last, I looked up, amazed and not a little proud of myself as well, I confess. But what a joy to be painting again.

The sketches were still rough but they were right. Gabriel lifted me off my feet with his good arm and kissed the hollow of my throat. "My Cecile, I knew you could do it. What's your secret?"

"My secret is my teacher, I think."

"No, You're quick. Quite so."

"What would St. Lucy say?"

"Encore." He kissed my throat again.

Now, I think back on those summer days when I was Gabriel's hands and I wonder if I had created a delicious fantasy. When I get to wondering too much, I take out the few sketches I set down on linen scraps and saved.

Though the drawings lack the grace and gift of Gabriel's work, my own sketches remain true. I remind myself that for one week he and I were one person: he the eyes, the voice, the teacher; and I, his fingers, his right hand.

We wandered about Chartres in the afternoons when the bakery's morning rush was past. We paused to watch the wheelwrights bend wood into hoops, and the coopers craft their barrels; we watched birds and trees and faces.

Gabriel told me what he noticed and I tried to draw these shapes into his copybook. Each day I learned more about line and form and balance in a sketch; my teacher remained a patient.

Never did I ask why we drew people from life; people who were not likely to appear in a cathedral's stained glass windows. My teacher did not say but I knew why. Gabriel was doing new work through me.

I understood so well, I feared for him. This matter would soon explode and I knew where. In a few days he would take his copybook to the forest studio, where his glass makers would render what he wished—including some traditional designs.

He honored me when he showed his sketches for enormous rose windows, lancet windows, and those with graceful Gothic arches. All had the marks of gift and grace and, yes, even glory. I do not think I say that only out of love.

Those sketches worried me not at all. It was the newer ones that did: they were balanced but more detailed, hardly simple. Too much, perhaps, for the eyes of men who were not artists?

All these designs had been surveyed and discussed, at first in private. Perhaps they were already compared with other offerings. Expectations would be lofty; no mistakes could creep in now.

Judgment day was drawing near and afterwards—what? A triumphant new beginning or a crushing finish. We would hear this judgment over dinner at our house; not the usual evening supper, but a feast, ten days away.

Then and there I must host a group of powerful men: the Bishop, his assistant, Father Louis, a scholar from the Cathedral School, two from the Cathedral's Chapter, and two likely sponsors. One of these, Jean Morrisot, would sit at my table. The absence of Bonnet was most regrettable.

I cloaked myself in false calm, but silently I kicked and cursed. A pox on these arrogant guests, I ranted to myself. Who were they to judge great art? At our household's expense, I might have added; this would be considerable, I knew.

The judges would look closely at the designs and drawings in Gabriel's copybook, we were told. The entire process seemed to me unspeakably and not a little overwhelming. Gabriel's work was extraordinary, I knew. Who else would see that, I wondered, now that Bonnet was gone?

We had to devise some other plans if the Bishop and his men did not share my opinion. But suppose all our plans failed? I could not bear to see Gabriel meet with such a disappointment—and live forever haunted by his father's reputation.

Each day, as I woke before the dawn, I asked myself: Is it good to love someone this much? The answer came to me one morning. What did it matter? Knowing wouldn't change a thing.

I turned my mind to questions with solid answers. What sort of fish to buy? What sort of fruit? How much honey, how much cream, how much wine? Which foods would foster pleasant thoughts, clear eyes, and open minds?

I dreaded this meal even as I planned it. Thrice I took the Lord's name in vein. Twice I cursed the guests' names. Once I confessed to cursing.

And as always, I wished that funeral procession, sad as it was, had never crossed a planted field. I know a bad omen when I see one.

■

Your ideas will not do, sir."

The Bishop set down his goblet.

"Then I withdraw my name." Gabriel set down his own goblet with a sharp clink.

"Let us not be quite so hasty, gentlemen." Morrisot continued to sip his wine.

"Let us not, indeed, most honored guests." My stepfather, hands trembling, opened a new bottle.

"Let him go to hell, that priest who shakes his head," Nicolette whispered in the pantry. "Shakes his head and eats, eats, eats."

"Let him pay for this feast, even if he is the Bishop's assistant. Father Louis has an appetite for food, not art." I whipped fresh cream as if it were somehow to blame for everything.

The dinner had gone wrong, terribly wrong, no matter how we tried to make it delightful to behold, delectable to eat, and deferential to our guests. As if those words were magic charms, I repeated them to myself, hoping my intentions would promote quick approval for Gabriel's designs.

Not only had he and I labored over every drawing in his copybook, Nicolette and I had spent a great deal of time and work on the feast—not to mention the matter of money spent.

Not to mention scouring the solar and the stairs, scrubbing stains with lye, starching our linens with potato skins and hanging up what must be dried: the top tablecloth, the second table cloth, the hand cloths, our aprons, tunics, shifts.

That was only the beginning of our labors. We polished knives; we polished floors, pans, platters. Not one chamberpot escaped our whisking cloths. Next we wiped out goblets, ewers, bowls, and we were nowhere near half-done.

Two days in advance we started on the meal itself: mincing, dicing, peeling. I chopped leeks with vicious energy. I beheaded fish with grim dispatch. I hacked a cabbage head in half. And then I looked around for something else to spear or skin. Finding nothing better, I pounded potatoes into pulp.

No simple crock of pottage for these guests, oh no. They had tomatoes stuffed with baby peas. Next, sautéed sole with grapes, buttered asparagus and pureed potato pies. An ample cheese tray; bread, of course. To finish, raspberry tarts with cream. Summer flowers on the table. Fragrant rush mats on the floor. To me, it all appeared to be a setting for superlatives.

And still the dinner was disastrous.

Gabriel's hand had healed well and remarkably fast, thanks to my aunt. That much could be said. In his copybook, Gabriel had set down a drawing for every opening, or "light," in an entire window. There was a precise rendering of each pane of glass. Pieced together they would make a whole.

We did not notice one torn seam in what we thought were seamless plans. So plain it was we missed the fatal flaw. Trapped within the confines of his copybook, most of Gabriel's designs looked cramped or crowded. Bold lines, rendered small, appeared confusing. I had to admit it: Much of the art's brilliance had been lost.

I had hoped the judges could imagine how Gabriel's work would look if it were drawn to scale. Clearly, this was not about to happen; not that night. If only we'd been able to afford enough paper, or even vellum, to display the work at its proper size.

Still, I had lain awake pondering this: Even if we'd had the perfect backgrounds and dimensions, were these men equipped to catch the genius of these images, created piece by piece, to form a whole.

On paper, doors and arches could make sense to a viewer; sculpture and statuary might. But who could grasp the power of transparent images—without any light behind them? Glass-makers could do this although they worked on flat and solid tables. Our guests, of course, lacked their eyes.

"Are these stock figures?" Morrisot asked.

"Or drawn from life?" The Bishop pressed.

"Both are here." Gabriel was firm.

"Each trade's confraternity will have figures." My stepfather burst into the discussion. "Some stock poses, like you call them. Others...how to put it... looser lines." He caught himself speaking out of turn. "I mean...begging your pardons, M'lords."

"I see," said Morrisot.

He did, I thought.

The others did not.

Those men were maddening to me: vigorous but vague in their objections; no suggestions, no specifics. Perhaps they thought Gabriel too young, —and too spare with compliments. Perhaps his designs were so detailed they baffled our guests; they never pretended to be artists.

To my surprise, our best hope lay with the one man I feared most: Jean Morrisot. He cared as deeply for those windows as did the clerics. But I knew he was a worldly man, long exposed to art he collected. I suspected he alone could visualize the outcome of Gabriel's drawings.

This I give to wintry Morrisot: his interest in this decision was not only for his own glory as a patron and a noted donor. In this man was the same love his brother had for beauty. This Bishop was a wise and holy soul but here, that was not enough.

Did he have an eye for art? Even if such a gift were his, could he convince the others? I wasn't sure he would want to try. How could he please them all? The bishop's desire to create harmony was obvious enough. I looked at Morrisot but couldn't read him. Nothing about that man was obvious.

Oddly enough, he seemed concerned about Gabriel, as a father might be for a son. I recalled that Morrisot had lost his only child, a boy; perhaps he saw that son in Gabriel. Then, too, the older man wanted glorious windows: God's loving gaze in glass.

"I am not yet satisfied."

At last, Father Louis, the Bishop's assistant, had spoken. He was a heavy man, thick about the waist, with tawny hair and eyes like silver buttons. How those eyes glowed at our food; how I wished those eyes would glow at Gabriel's designs.

"Show us that blue you spoke of so highly. We have seen not a hint of it." Father Louis challenged him now. "And why do your designed so...how to put it...crowded? How much can one take in?"

"Perhaps more than you think," Gabriel dared to say. "Why is there no place for what you call 'detailed windows'?"

"You will confuse the people." The Bishop's assistant selected a piece of candied ginger.

"Confuse? Not so easily. They deserve more credit than you give. Bonnet would agree."

"Bonnet, rest his soul, had a short stay with us." Father Louis chose a glazed almond. "I fear you may shorten your own."

"Afraid?" Gabriel's voice sharpened. "Are you? Afraid of something new?"

"Like blue?" Morrisot gave a tight smile.

"Blue will soon come."

"When, pray tell, is soon?"

"Art cannot be rushed."

"In this case, it has to be."

There was another of those stifling silences. The clink of cutlery and the flow of wine became huge and weighty sounds, too loud for this chamber.

Nicolette and I appeared with more tarts, and still more wine, as if with sweets and drink we might somehow change the atmosphere. The table, under the Bishop's hefty elbows, seemed to wobble.

I hoped we had set it properly upon its legs. On one side of it, we had mixed and diced and sliced. Then we had turned the table, so the smooth side faced up, as it did now, beneath the two tablecloths and the wilting garlands of roses.

As if this made any difference.

No one was charmed by the food, the wine, the table or, sadly, the copybooks.

I exchanged looks with Gabriel.

He nodded when I raised an eyebrow.

He and I would have to put our next plan into action—a daring plan but the only one we had.

It was time.

We must begin.

■

C ome," Gabriel invited our guests.
He waited at the cellar steps.
I felt like a child trying to keep her balance on a sloping garden wall. And then, as I had hoped, the Bishop, with Morrisot, followed their host down the stairs beyond the bakery into my "pastry room."

There, this afternoon, we had welcomed the forest's glass-makers who brought new glass panels, stained and formed to fit into a model window of their Master's own design.

Gabriel had inked the outlines of each shape on a sheet of cloth, stretched across a long wooden frame. This notion had come to me from my aunt's apothecary shop—and the stretcher, or litter, leaning on her wall.

My aunt had widened the litter last night and given it long legs. Also she had crafted it to a precise size: Not the size to bear a body—but the size to bear one section of a stained glass window's panel, still in pieces, edges smoothed.

The glass-makers had set these on shelves while I had set unlit lamps on the cellar floor, underneath the linen litter. The rest fell to Gabriel. I only prayed the lamps, when lit, would not set our high "table" on fire.

Perish the thought.

"This is but a sample, a model," Gabriel began. "I have planned another, larger St. Joseph window with many scenes. Tonight you see what kind work awaits you in my smaller designs. Here is what you can't see in the copybook. Soon my figures will leap toward you."

Now Gabriel took a flat oval of white glass in his hands and placed it on the cloth. This white piece, I knew, went where a figure's face was meant to be. My glazier gathered other glass fragments and presented them to the Bishop himself. "Your Excellency must be first."

"First? For what, may I ask?"

"Place the glass as you see fit."

"But why? I don't understand."

"Serious business, Your Excellency."

"We shall see," the Bishop said. "I'll try."

Leaning over the long table, he set several glass shapes so they fit Gabriel's inked outline on the cloth. Suddenly, it seemed, the pieces came together in the form of a workman's red tunic.

Now Morrisot was invited to choose another slice of glass and set it in place. This he did, with ease, fitting the shape to its proper space. And then another; then one more.

A plump hand reached out as Father Louis picked a triangle of purple glass. Father Mark, from the Cathedral School, moved with care as he selected a crescent shape. Soon the puzzle had captivated each man in the gathering.

Long they were at this intriguing challenge. Taking turns, each stepped forward to add a bit of color, a fraction of a form. A piece of green glass here, a touch of saffron there. A rectangle, a circle, a border of diamond shapes.

Before our eyes it finally emerged: an image of that holy carpenter, St. Joseph, compelling and complete. He had something like a "stock" pose but I knew the figure was first drawn from an unsuspecting workman in the town.

I felt a strange sensation running down my spine, as if someone had poured cool water there. Right there, in the baker's cellar, I was watching a cathedral's stained glass figure come into being.

Gabriel reached for his jar of special paint; I knew it was made from ground lead, gum arabic— and urine. Our guests did not. He took up his brush, dipped it in the jar and stood before us, painting human hair and features on the white oval of glass.

As we watched, that oval became a face, its eyes alive and watchful, looking out as if they could see us. The artist's hand was swift: St. Joseph's features emerged as he glanced up at us. There was a gasp, a murmur, then an awed silence.

Gabriel gave the paint brush to the Bishop, who was asked to add a chin to the glass face. I saw the paint brush settle into the cleric's hand and there it remained steady. His Excellency hesitated only for a moment before he began.

Squinting, he rendered every stroke with sober precision. When the Bishop handed the brush back, Gabriel painted hair, a beard, an expressive mouth, clever hands and folds in the tunic. The judges stood hushed, watching how a gifted artist could conjure a character from air—and give him life.

The same process was repeated for a smaller figure, enclosed in a half-circle beneath the first—this one was a banker, for contrast. He, too, seemed to look out at us when his eyes were painted and his cloak fell in graceful folds. At last the window panel was finished, including its decorative border of linked diamond shapes.

Time for me to move, and fast.

As we'd planned, I blew out all the work lights in the room and lit the eight small lamps on the floor under the "table," well below the cloth. First the cloth brightened. Then the glass itself took on a magical tinge. It grew. It glowed. It sharpened. Abruptly, both figures seemed to breathe. Even the dour Father Louis let out another gasp.

For a long while we stood staring at what lay before us: those full-scale figures, rich with color, radiant with light, nearly alive. Everyone stood mute and moved.

I saw a flush on Morrisot's pale face and a glimmer in his eyes. "Beautiful," he said. "Perfect proportions, original forms. The right colors. And that sophisticated diamond border. My compliments to this amazing artist."

Gabriel bowed in thanks, then turned to the Bishop. "Your Excellency. You seek the tradesmen's confraternities as donors?"

"Indeed, Sir. You hear aright."

"Might the tradesmen be pictured in their windows? One or two figures, representing all their brothers? Stock poses, some of them, with my own touches and expressions. A way to 'sign' their work."

"Just so," the Bishop said. "Precisely."

"M'sieur Dufort, how many would that be?"

"Forty-two confraternities, I make it."

"Forty-two groups of donors," Morrisot announced as if the thing was done. "Such gifts will be of great value. We always need more funds. These additions may hasten my hope: walls of stained glass windows."

"This is a most pleasing outcome." the Bishop nodded. "Sometimes a bit of...strain...flaws our relations with the confraternities. Mere humans, are we not? " He glanced at my stepfather. "Here I see a way to ease such strain. Of course, we must meet again to make a firm decision."

"That is easily arranged," Morrisot's voice quickened in the cellar. "Here is a fine way to draw the trades into this work." He almost smiled. "Of course we welcome them. If all goes as I now hope, much good will come of this."

"I tell you, sir." The Bishop looked directly at Gabriel. "Mighty work was done here tonight, one night alone. We are most grateful to you. But tell me this: How will this glass stay in place?"

"Fitted into grooved lead cames," Gabriel told him. "Strong ones. They hold it all together."

The Bishop reached forward and touched the glowing colored surfaces before him. "Miraculous," he murmured, more to himself than anyone else. "Yes. We must take this matter up with the Cathedral Chapter in the morning. I can promise nothing yet, of course. You understand, I'm sure."

"The Cathedral School should view this. Others, as well." Morrisot waved his thin hand toward the stained glass display. "This cellar must become a gallery tomorrow. If other visitors might lay down the glass as we did, they will understand what's in that copybook.

"Of course, of course," my stepfather intervened. "My cellar is yours. *Our* cellar is yours."

"We meet directly after Mass," the Bishop reminded us. "Tomorrow morning in my study. Late afternoon is a good time to escort others here. The light outside will fade, the light in here will glow."

"All will be ready." I spoke out before I thought what I was doing. "Everything prepared."

Our guests stared at me.

"You are—?" One of them asked.

"The baker's daughter," I stepped back. "I met many of you gentlemen at His Excellency's banquet."

"She presented a confection, a model palace," Father Louis said. "I recall M'amselle Dufort."

"As do I." Morrisot looked at me.

"You may not know this," I added. "M'sieur Gabriel worked with a wounded hand, his drawing hand, to design all you see here and all you saw upstairs. Rare dedication is another prize."

To Gabriel I curtsied, wondering if he would start to laugh. I myself had to stop the laughter and relief fizzing up inside me. The others spoke their thanks and admiration; no apologies, of course. It was as if the disastrous dinner had not happened.

~~~

After our guests had gone, we quenched the floor lamps and finished off the wine. My stepfather, flushed and drunk and pleased, staggered off to bed. After three drinks in the pantry, Nicolette was a bit unsteady as we cleaned up the feast's remains. Soon she groped her way to her attic sleeping place. Our house was still at last.

Gabriel turned and pulled me into his arms. For a long while, there were no words for us, only that tight embrace in the dim pantry.

"You did it," he said at last.

"Oh no. It was your work."

"My love, it was you." He pressed me against him and we were longer still in the pantry where its sweets and tarts tempted us not in the least.

Finally, we forced ourselves to trudge downstairs so we could wrap the glass and put it away. The stairs were narrow and Gabriel went behind me with his hands on my shoulders. Between us hung a charmed silence, fragrant as cut grass.

This is how it would be, I thought. This is how it could be. It was as if we were a longtime married couple, readying our own house for the night. How far we had come quite far from those dark ruins.

"It will all come right," I said. "The windows will be the way you want them. Some stock poses, yes, but with your touch, your details, and some drawn from life. A fine mingling, I'd say."

"Admit it. You told me so." He kissed the back of my neck. "Go on. Tell me I'm hard-headed."

"We're well-matched there, love."

"More donors. More designs."

"More repute for you and Chartres." I was feeling giddy from the wine and the victory and Gabriel's nearness, probably all three. "You will shine, M'sieur le Glazier."

"Call me that again," he ruffled my hair. "*Curtsy* to me, for God's sake, and I will—"

"You will—?" I leaned against him.

"—confine you to bed directly."

"Yours?" I realized I was drunk.

"Indefinitely." Gabriel was sober.

We doused the lights, all save one we used to find our way back up the stairs. The cellar sank back into its ordinary form and shape—a room so familiar, I could find my way through it in the dark.

I noticed its usual smells of yeast and damp, honey and flour. Tomorrow, we would close its shutters and it would become a gallery. Never will I understand how the simple and the splendid sometimes flow together.

Gabriel led me up the stairs and into the solar, where we collapsed upon the widest bench, but when I kissed his fingertips, he winced and I drew back.

"You have overworked your hand, I fear."

"I want to touch you, Cecile, here, there...."

"May your hand heal swiftly," I sighed.

He went to his room, I to mine, and we twisted in our separate sheets. He turned; I turned.

"Cecile?" His whisper floated down the hall.

"What's that?" My stepfather's voice.

Prudence won out over passion.

Finally, I drifted off into a dusky sleep where Gabriel and I walked through a purple meadow on a silver path to our house: a house of glowing glass.

How fragile it would prove to be.

■

Imagine one night of a thousand torches and a thousand stars, of beer and blessings and a breeze—these were near; these were now.

So it was for those of us who formed the great procession from the stone quarries of Bérchères to the cathedral's ruins, and briefly, all of us were one. Rarely, I have noticed, what is lost is found. Now we were finding our lost cathedral.

And so it happened that in the summer of 1194, the people of Chartres, young and old, rich and poor, men and women, burgher and peasant, went out to that great gray field of quarried stone and drew from the place its heavy fruit, loading it onto carts and drays and barrows.

Every ox and mule and horse in the town was there, hitched to those carts, and we, more than 1,000 townspeople, yoked ourselves to those carts as well. These we pulled ourselves; in fact, we were hauling our new cathedral into Chartres. I glanced around the quarry, hard-edged, even harsh, but just then it looked rich: a silver meadow in the slanting light.

Even without the Master of Works, the masons had already cut new stones, stacked upon each other. Not the heaviest of stones, perhaps, but sacred to us; signs of things to come.

Men could swing them up by ropes to carts and drays, while smaller stones were placed into that clever new invention, widely used now, the wheel barrow; these the children pushed.

The sun lay long and low across the quarry on that summer evening, and the work went on till dark. I still remember the dank smell of stone and its fine dust, and the ripe aroma of so many animals, and the warmth of the crowd we formed.

As ever, what I recall best is Gabriel—and our own yoke. I recall the way we leaned forward as if we were one, moving slowly in that long and storied line of carts. I see it still:

The procession forming, strung together starting from the quarry and lumbering down the road. The bright colors of tunics and caps, reds and greens and purples; grays and browns and blacks of straining horses and donkeys.

With torches, groomsmen walk beside each cart and men and women with their heads through oxen's yokes. We want to give this gift of our sweat to our cathedral; we want to honor the Blessed Virgin Mary in this way.

This is a bursting forth of our gratitude to God for preserving our relic, Mary's childbirth tunic, the *Sancta Camisa,* and the cathedral foundations themselves, still stable, penetrating twenty-five feet below the ground.

And now I am pulling a cart for what I might have well destroyed. I never thought that I, a woman, could not labor so. Other women, some stronger, some slighter, were hitched to carts before me and behind me.

Looking back, I see myself standing in the quarry with Gabriel. The yoke is put over our heads by two dray men and—of all people—personally directed by Jean Morrisot, gaunt but determined.

He has paired us, yoked together. Now he watches the two of us with that odd glimmer in his eyes. As always, the sight of Morrisot sends me a series of chills. I have not forgotten how he stood back and watched Gabriel and me that one night in the cathedral's ruins

Nor can I forget the way this spear of a man smiled then—the same smile I see now: Secretive and stealthy as a thief. As if he somehow participated in our love. Shuddering, I quickly turn away from M'sieur Jean Morrisot.

He, the Bishop's brother, watches over this procession, although the Bishop himself presides and leads the way. Our cart is light enough and I feel the loop of wood over my shoulders, connecting me, Cecile, with Gabriel.

It seems quite right that we are yoked together. He glances at my face and then away as

Morrisot looks us over, nodding to himself and then to us, bestowing his frosty smile.

"This will do quite well," he says in a strange and quiet voice. To us? To himself? To the crowd? I did not know. "Quite well indeed." The words are pleasing but their tone is ominous.

"An easy load." Gabriel says. "No fear."

Morrisot regards us again and I hear the echo of another meaning in his voice. "Not too much for you, M'amselle Cecile?"

"Not in the least, sir." I flare up, defiant.

"Well-matched," Gabriel says and Morrisot gives him a sharp look. "We start now."

"So I notice." The merchant pauses, then turns to me. "You have a strong young man to pull with you, Cecile Dufort. M'sieur Gabriel, give due care to her and to your hands. They just may prove valuable to us." Morrisot's face shuts like a Bible after mass. He moves nearer, then turns away.

I do not know what he is playing at but I doubt he does anything by chance. Crafty, canny, calculating, he has thought out each detail, each step of this parade. He has even set several young men with crops walking up and down the line of carts, keeping the horses in order. All appears well-planned.

Now the aging man walks with pride beside the carts. With humans pulling them, as well as animals, we can double the amount of stone that will begin the new cathedral. This is an unexpected cause for celebration. We call it, "The Cult of the Carts."

Nobility and peasants pull together; craftsmen pull with the clergy. Were it not for the nature of this pilgrimage, tensions would surface, no doubt. I turn back to Gabriel, who is flushed with rage at Morrisot —for many reasons.

We both feel beholden to the older man and resent this to the bone. Then there is the unfinished matter of the marriage suit. It is a complex and confusing web indeed.

Now my partner looks at me and his face relaxes. As he turns, I feel his movements through the yoke. It is somehow sensual to be joined like this; we can feel each breath, each motion of the other. In the long low amber light, we smile.

Ahead of us, the Bishop is blessing the pilgrimage and the new stones drawn toward Chartres. Amid a chorus of "Amens,"we begin our journey. This, I think, is a new way of walking hand in hand; it is one of the strangest feeling in my life.

We are indeed on pilgrimage. The sky arches over us and the road reels out before us and I hear chanting on the air, behind us and ahead. *Gloria in Excelsis Deo,* people murmur *Non nobis, Dómine...* Not us, Lord. To You the Glory.

Part of one another, Gabriel and I, we are also part of something larger than ourselves. We know this, we see this plain, as if the line of we make is embroidered on the dimming sky and on the minds of all who walk here.

If anyone glimpses the procession from afar that evening, he or she would see a long series of people moving at a steady pace as one: silhouettes set against amber fields and the great bowl of sky, every cart and barrow flanked by flaring torches.

How small we would appear; how brave. What we carry now can build so little, that we know. The workmen will do this work again and again, through many years. This is a beginning only—but like all beginnings and all births, there is a kind of humble splendor and daring and danger to it.

The sky is fading.

Abruptly I hear a panicked horse neighing behind us. I cannot tell how far away it is nor can I to turn around to look. The sound is growing louder— now the whinny rises to scream; I hear the horse stomping and striking the ground.

Frightened by some noise, the horse's hooves drum faster: now the rhythm of a canter, then a gallop, and carts lumber left and right, trying to get off the road. The young grooms are running but they may not be fast or strong enough to stop this spreading frenzy.

The frightened horse zigzags, breaking free of its reins and driver, a white-faced man with a load of sharp-angled stones. Other horses catch the panic, rearing, breaking loose. Human voices, shrill and loud, are screaming now. The groomsmen, paired and alone, still struggle to calm the bucking horses.

Together we walk faster but the yoke is clumsy and our load seems heavier than it was before. At our backs, the noise heightens. We move faster still for fear of being trampled but others, behind us, quicken their pace.

They are pressing toward us, closer, closer still. If we don't get off this road, we might veer off balance or fall in the dust. Our cart could easily roll over us. Breathing hard, I feel my heart banging against my ribs.

"Cecile, hold on," Gabriel calls.

"I am," I call back. "What now?"

"Go left. Can you?"

"Yes." My voice shakes. I lean and stretch as far as I can but the yoke resists and the weighted cart will not shift. The procession threatens to break up; more carts crowd nearer. Someone yells at us to hurry on ahead but we are almost running now.

From nowhere, it seems, a silken sleeve brushes our yoke. "Stand still," Jean Morrisot commands us. "I'll not lose either one of you just yet."

With him are two of the young grooms. At his command, they take the yoke off our shoulders and, hand in hand, we dart from the road and into a border of weeds and grass.

"Cecile," Gabriel says. "You're hurt?"

"Only shaken," I tell him. "And you?"

"Mortified. Didn't want his rescue."

"Nor I. Still, we're safe, love, together."

"Yes. But owing him. Hate that."

"So do I. I'm praying he'll forget."

"Maybe. In this mess. Look there."

At last, the groomsmen have begun to calm the horses and their drivers. Others, unyoked like us, stand up now, drawing long breaths, brushing themselves off.

However jarred they may be, they look determined to go on. Some are even reaching for their yokes. Slowly, Morrisot moves up and down the road, speaking with the people while the grooms go on setting all to rights.

Morrisot's unmistakable power outweighs his frailty. He commands a fresh effort and renewed calm. Of course, I remember: this is "his" procession and he will not let it fail. Before Morrisot can offer us assistance, we rise and take up our own yoke as well.

The line is assembled as before. Slowly, then, the carts and yokes begin to move forward. Relief breeds an uncanny calm; it falls over us like a spell or blessing. The Bishop, calm himself, urges us on. Voices rise again: *Gloria in Excelsis Deo....*

I am sore, I am aching, I am thirsty, and my tunic falls below my shoulders, its seams split. Even so, I can never regret our part in this procession, nor our place with these staunch townsfolk.

We move on with the others, flanked by torches, until we have reached the cathedral grounds. The stones will be unloaded by strong masons tomorrow. Now we all gather to kneel together before the remnants of our old cathedral.

The Bishop intones a blessing I can barely hear but his words have a cadence like a chant. Yet, even there, in that sacred space, I sense that something, somewhere, is wrong, but we will not find out in time.

In the town, as we celebrate our part in the new construction, an evildoer in the forest relishes his part in the destruction of Gabriel's newest and bluest store of glass.

■

A night of celebration and catastrophe. A night of minstrels and troubadours, dancing and music—and intrigue.

A night of ale, too much, perhaps; for others, not enough. A night of acrobats, flipping like children's toys and leaping through the air, while jugglers' colored balls make looping patterns, caught by the torchlight.

Minstrels prance about, showing off their reds and greens. Singing, they play their gitterns, fiddles and what we called a "symphony:" a wooden box with keys along one side and on one end, a crank. This has always made me laugh, ever since I was a child.

I hear laughter now and still more song. There is a dancing bear, its collar tightly leashed, and a prancing dog wearing a collar of bright bells; they jingle as the dog jumps through a hoop, to a burst of cheers and applause.

Sweets and cider pass from hand to hand. Thirsty work was done and so we drink cider— but I cannot eat. Gabriel looks worried but I can't explain. Why am I so unsettled, so distant from this scene? Why am I waiting for some kind of shock? I cannot find the answer; not here, not yet.

Amid all of these delights, there are spying eyes. Nicolette watches Gabriel. The Bishop watches his assistant. The assistant watches the Reverend Monsignor. Morrisot squints at me. My stepfather peers at pretty girls. I catch him drawing Morrisot toward him in a conversation I cannot quite hear—I do not want to hear.

I see Henri Dufort, perhaps for the first time, in a new way. Though his efforts always seem grounded in self-interest, I see how hard he must have struggled with his life; his climb to wealth.

Things have not come easily to this man. He has made his own way and if he has to bend rules and play the fox, I understand for the first time. I can't forget his beatings or his willingness to sell me as a bride. For the moment, though, I can forgive.

Now gusts of laughter blend with the start of a chain dance, unreeling before us, snaking through the torchlight. The chain forms a circle now, a slow ring dance moving like a stately wheel, and as it whirls, it goes faster, spinning in the light.

It is all a blur of blues and reds and yellows; skirts swinging, tunics flashing by. Pieces of another stained glass window are forming in Gabriel's mind, I think; I know.

But more than a window fills his thoughts. He stands outside the circle and looks at me; I stand outside the circle some distance away. The night leans over us as we edge closer to each other, hidden by the twirling ribbon of dancers.

We move until our hands reach out and meet and clasp. I recall the holy vows we made on holy ground, in the presence of a witness: Jean Morrisot, oddly enough. I will go with Gabriel tonight, I decide, even before he can whisper through the dark, through the music: "Come with me, my Cecile, the shed, the woods. Come now."

We go by separate routes, threading through the narrow, empty streets and lanes, just beyond the town to his glass-makers' forest clearing and his shed. This is safer, we think, than my stepfather's house; safer, farther from the town. No one seems to be about; only the trees whisper.

Tonight I feel it right that we should be together in Gabriel's shed hung with all those chiming fragments of blue glass—not the right blue he seeks, but blue all the same.

He pulls me into his arms and holds me and his breath catches in his throat. His hands are in my hair and his mouth clings to mine. The night sounds of the forest fall away and there is only this small circle we make together. And then he open the door to the shed.

We jolt to a stop on the threshold.

Lifting our lamps, we stand in shocked silence and disbelief. For a moment we can only stare at what lies before us: every piece of blue glass has been wrenched from the ceiling and smashed against the ground. It is as if a slice morning sky has come crashing through the roof and shattered there, glinting in our lamp's light.

Shards and splinters of blue glass spangle Gabriel's straw pallet, his drawing board and his table of tools. Looking up, we see that each string has been wrenched off its nail on the ceiling and the tangled strings themselves lie amid the rubble.

"Keep back," he warns.

"Who would do this—?"

"Damn and blast."

As Gabriel wades into the shed, the shattered glass crunches like gravel beneath his shoes. He swings his light here and there, looking for some sign of an intruder crouching in a corner, someone waiting for us, perhaps.

Among the sparkling debris, we both see something that is not a string but a rope of a good length. We lift it out and hold it up before lanthorns. light. To me, in my alarmed state, the thing looks like a hangman's noose, a snake—but I know better.

There is no mistaking what it is: the belt or cincture of a monk, with its crucifix still attached. I make some noise in my throat but Gabriel does not hear me. He is already moving.

I have never seen such fury on his face, like wind roiling water. Still gripping the rope-belt, he makes his way toward me, through the doorway, and out into night, suddenly dangerous, at my back.

I wheel around. The invader could yet be near. Lifting my lanthorn, I scan the darkness of the woods. Behind me, in the shed, something stirs. I signal to Gabriel; our eyes dart about until there is another noise. We see him then, half-hidden by a table, the crouching figure of a man.

"Stay here," Gabriel whispers.

"Keep safe for God's sake."

"Don't move, Cecile."

He wheels around as the man springs out of his hiding place: under a table. As he hurls himself at us, his strange laughter flecks the air. I see a flash of the monk's habit now.

Above it I make out a toad-like face and snarling mouth, spitting at us both. Gabriel grabs the monk but the smaller man wrenches his arm free. They struggle, grappling with each other, overturning stools and then the table, and the monk keeps spitting, "*Sinners, sinners.*"

Strong and agile, he raises both fists to strike, but Gabriel grabs the monk's wrists and throws him down. Shouting like a madman, the robed brother leaps back into the fight and then the two men are rolling on the ground.

For what seems a long time, they wrestle there; the monk's ugly shape revealed, bent and twisted beneath his graying hair. Gabriel throttles the intruder, gets him down and pins him to the ground. At last the intruder goes limp.

"Is he dead?" My voice is small.

"Far from dead." Gabriel stands up.

"And you?"

"Far from dead." His voice is dry.

"You're hurt, I think."

"Not this time." He sounds grim.

He grabs the monk by the cowl and drags him into the night and the monk spatters blood and spits broken teeth and curses. Before he can fight back, we have him twined with his own cincture and so trussed, we march him toward town and straight into the center of the celebration.

Spying Gabriel and the monk, the dancers skid to a stop. The gitterns and lutes fall silent. Revelry hangs like an unfinished song on the dark air. Instantly, the Bishop and his brother are before us and Gabriel hurls the monk down at their feet. Others gather now with torches; the *bâilli* hurries near, as he does whenever law and order lapse.

With unexpected strength, the monk breaks his bonds, kicks out at Morrisot and growls at the Bishop—poor choices, both. The *bâilli* and his men grab the small man. As they do, he tries to bite his captors' hands. A collective gasp rises from the crowd. Before the monk is trussed again, he points at us all.

"Sinners," he shouts. "Idolaters."

"Who sent you?" The *bâilli* barks.

"God sent me. To punish you."

"God? Or someone here on earth?"

"God, I say, the God you blaspheme."

"Chevan sent you." Morrisot accuses him.

"My abbot knows nothing of my mission."

"Did he inspire it? Speak now."

"He would not disapprove." The monk rakes us with his gaze. "You people make an *idol* of your cathedral. You want to be admired for its beauty. You forget the poor who need the funds you raise."

"Shut your mouth," the *bâilli* barks.

"And you—" the monk turns on Gabriel. "You with your pretty glass, your pretty girl. You are not a holy man."

"Enough,"the *bâilli* roars.

We explain what happened in the shed. "If I'd hung the first of our cathedral windows there," Gabriel adds, "they too would be splinters. I can't work under threat. I won't put my men in danger." He looks at me. "Or anyone else."

"Of course." Morrisot is flushed with rage.

"I will see to Abbot Chevan," the Bishop gazes over us all. "And I trust the *bâilli* will see to this vandal, this...invader. Monk or not, until tomorrow, he is under guard. When we return him to his monastery, his abbot must discipline him."

I watch Gabriel's face. I see rage mix with triumph there; a bit of that boy he'd once been who scrapped with the others. I also see a bruise above his eye; the blood on him is from the monk.

None of this is lost upon the torch-lit crowd. The Bishop himself claps Gabriel on the back with big splayed hands. How different are these two men, I think; they balance each other out, somehow, but that is an illusion, I know.

I watch their faces, one rough and red as roasted beef, one fine-boned and tanned. These are faces nobody would see in a century from now, nor down all the centuries ahead, but those two men would always be here, in each stone, each pane of glass to come.

The Bishop is a worldly man, yet a pious one. Like his brother, Morrisot, he is dark-eyed but his eyes are larger, kinder, beneficent. Now the Bishop steps forward and gazes around at all of us. The torches sputter in the silence before the Bishop speaks again and this time, with great force.

"This cathedral will be raised to the glory of God and to Our Lady." He crosses himself and goes on. "First and foremost it stands as an offering and a tribute—not an idol. Its inspiration flows from the Divine and not proud men." That last is for the monk who spits at the Bishop.

"Empty words. Idolaters you are."

"Nor could we be," the Bishop's tone is steady. "This cathedral tells the story of God's people, from creation to the end of time. We only try to capture it in glass and stone." He turns to the monk. "Tell that to your Father Abbot."

The monk snarls something but his mouth is bound. The *bâilli's* men drag him away and the circle of torches draws around Gabriel.

"Our work is our free offering to the Holy One," the Bishop goes on, his eyes brushing every face. "This great church will go unsigned by any of us. Chartres cathedral belongs to God. Near holiness there always lurks great danger."

■

D anger in blowing glass is breathing fire.

I feared this for Gabriel's sake when I went with him to his cauldrons in the woods. Danger always crouched inside a flame—that I knew all too well. And yet, I knew this man was seasoned, gifted, careful: a Master of his art, his craft.

I would watch him with his blow-pipe and think of his lips on mine. I would see him as a lover, a magician, and a flute player. It was thrilling and unnerving and confusing to watch him work.

When he did, he would dip a blow-pipe into a crucible of molten glass, then turn the pipe in his hands until he got the right-sized "gather," or mass, on the other end. Next he would take the pipe from his mouth and hold it just beside his lips, so he could breathe in fresh air for a moment.

I found that I breathed in and out with him whenever he did this, as if the force of my caring could protect him: he who needed none, at least in this case. After sending an air bubble into the "gather," he would shape the mass with his tools until it formed a long cylinder. I saw Gabriel reheat the glass while he worked it. His hands were deft as he took off the bottom of the cylinder.

How fast he was as he opened one end of it with a small round piece of wood; then the other end was opened. My eyes could hardly keep up with him as he turned to his ovens and heated the glass again, this time to flatten it into a sheet. Finally this would be cooled, annealed, and cut—with a red-hot iron. I always looked away while he did this last.

While Gabriel worked, his concentration was so intense, it was a force I could feel, like a light around him. After the glass was cut, Gabriel painted in details, then fired it all again. Exhausting, this process, to me; exciting to him.

As the windows were designed, Gabriel would soon allot most of their rendering to his various assistant glass-makers. For now, he wanted to "feel the glass" as he dreamed the windows into being.

I was so intent upon the danger from the glass and flame, I did not notice peril coiling in our workspace and our house itself. Why would I? Our luck seemed to be running fair of late. Like a hopeful fool, I dared to trust it.

What a relief: Gabriel went back to designing, this time in a traditional way; even so, it always seemed new and magical to me. I watched as he inscribed precise lines into the surface of chalked tables—paper was far too expensive and difficult to come by; most of it had to be ordered from mills in Spain. Gabriel used his few precious sheets sparingly and only for finished work.

"What about parchment?" I asked.

"Too expensive, wrong kind of surface."

"The monks have it, don't they?"

"No monk here." He kissed my hand—and gently removed it from his drawing table. "Parchment, after all, is dried sheeps' skin. Or pigs' skin. When I turn parchment pages, I'm turning a sow's flanks."

"Funny, yes?" Nicolette in the doorway.

"Where did you come from?" I jumped.

"Only passing by," Nic said. "Your stepfather called me to the bakery. While you work here today, he is shorthanded."

This was not true, I knew. Instead, I suspected the two of them were picking up an old flirtation.

"I saw you standing there." Gabriel was abrupt with Nicolette. "Several minutes, it was."

"Your drawing so interests me."

"I see." He turned back to it.

"Ironing next," I reminded Nicolette.

"Of course." She flounced away.

"The girl is harmless," I told Gabriel.

"Sure of that, Cecile?" He frowned.

"I am. She flirts. But she's a friend."

The first week we ran out of chalk so I prepared wooden boards covered in a flour paste spread to the right thickness; on this Gabriel could inscribe his new designs. Gabriel used a sharp pointed tool, something like a stylus. This left patterns that seemed ghostly; almost invisible to me.

Then, as I had seen him do before, he would take a shell filled with ashes and, holding it above the inscribed board, he would dust it with that fine black powder, then blow the powder off. Caught in these lines, the powder made the drawing appear. Gabriel then painted it in black or red.

No matter how often I saw this happen, it struck me afresh and amazed me. It was as if the drawing hid with the flour paste, or in the board itself, and he was cutting down to it, freeing it to come forth under his deft hands.

My paste-boards worked well and I could bake them easily; they dried to the right thickness and, more stable than chalk, such humble stuff became Gabriel's preferred drawing surfaces.

"All of this design work reminds me of making pastry," I said. "Yeast working in dough, so mysterious the way it rises. That must be how ideas rise in your mind." I cleared some tables for him and lifted my own small scales to move them.

"Stop." His voice was abrupt. "Like that."

I stood there on the cellar floor, my hair in a vague knot, my workaday green skirt soiled, feeling foolish as I held this humble measuring tool.

Even so, poised as he directed, I stood with the scales in my right hand. He was seeing something I could not imagine but his face was intent. His gaze, like sword, was aimed at my outline. Then he reached out for a board and one of his sharp tools.

"Turn, Cecile. Face me."

"Like this? Straight on?"

"Just that way." He hand moved.

"And these?" I held the scales.

"Can you lift them higher?"

I raised them and felt their weight and knew, then, he had broken through to a picture. This one must show Libra, with her scales, for the Zodiac Window. Libra—as a person, carrying her symbol but not trapped inside it. A human image, I realized, tapped the talent of such a personal and sensitive artist.

Now he was drawing faster, his hand sure and deft. From his board, the image was emerging, inscribed first, then dusted over with the ashes from the mussel shells. Then, when the ash was brushed away, it revealed, fully formed, his "Lady Libra." The Church could approve it—or not.

"Libra is right for you, Cecile," he said that night. "You keep me balanced. How I need that."

I did not feel balanced, watching him. I knew everything depended on the work he did here and now. This would lead to samples he must again present. 176 windows to design; most as the clergy wished. Even so, this commission was a prize, a plum, a pearl of great price.

Gabriel's small copybook was filled with designs, new and old, but he still had competitors. Even so, I knew, the best designs were his. The books were growing. And they grew thicker still.

Time was our opponent, our obsession now. It tested us and teased us and tightened around us every day.

At night we labored as the town slept. I stopped an hour before dawn when I had to bake the bread. In the afternoons, we rested in our separate rooms. So aware of Gabriel's nearness, I did not often —if ever—sleep soundly. We lived together, touching, kissing, talking, working. And how hard we tried to be "virtuous."

Morrisot came by from time to time, always at night, to ask after the work's progress. As far as I could tell, the neighbors saw nothing of what we were about; at least they did not question us.

Meanwhile, I put my trust in Nicolette for needed secrecy. She watched out for us, or so I thought, and fiercely guarded Gabriel. If she could have a moment to talk with him she glowed; if I came in, she pouted. But that was Nicolette—and as far as I could remember, always loyal, despite her variable moods: they were always shifting.

After every storm of temper, her remorse was real, and she did well in keeping the house—a task I never could have managed on my own just then. There were too many other things for me to manage: working in the cellar, making bread, coating boards and tables and assisting Gabriel.

The first day we went into the cellar, he had turned to me with an urgent question.

"Where should I start? So many Bible stories go into these windows." He shook his head. "The clergy has the largest say. Theologians, too, from the Cathedral School. I'll try some suggestions."

"Did the Bishop not request ideas?"

"Indeed—how I chafe against that."

"The artist should have his say." I was firm.

"A set of windows for Our Lady, of course. One with many panels for St. Joseph, another for Mary Magdalen. Noah. Adam and Eve...." Gabriel let out a growl of frustration. "The Zodiac Window: baffling to me." Gabriel ran his hand through his hair.

I looked at him, perched on a stool, set against a wall of baker's tools; they hung from the rack behind his head. I looked at the dough rising in the jute baskets along the shelves to his left and right and then I looked back to Gabriel. I was glad to have him here, and safe, rather than blowing glass out in the forest.

We had heard of glass-makers who were blinded when they added colored salts at the wrong strength and the glass blew up. Each tinted addition had its special properties—and risks.

Cobalt was a poison that could loose arsenic fumes; artisans' hated working with it. Just as I learned how to color pastry, now I learned Gabriel colors. It pleased him to describe their ingredients.

"Reds," he said.

He opened a chest of clay jars.

"Gold filings," he pointed to one jar.

I looked at the gleaming dust within.

"Blood." He pointed to another jar.

I gasped and he smiled, amused.

"Insect blood, 'Cochineal,' " he added.

"That makes red?"

"Carmine red."

Next he pointed at two other jars: one held copper filings to make green, the other held mercury refined, he said, with white sulphur. These he mixed together in a bottle and soon yellow smoke rose out of the vessel. Gabriel moved the bottle gently the yellow smoke turned red and then violet.

Each color had its own beauty and, one might say, a personality. Watching him at work, I was once again reminded of a wizard, a magician—or my grandmother and aunt, those wise apothecaries.

"Can't win my lady in a joust." His smiled. "Hope magic will do as well."

"You won weeks ago," I told him.

"Yellows come from these." He touched other jars. "Saffron. Gold leaf. Oh yes, and urine."

I peered into a jar of pigment nuggets, Indian Yellow. "Here is orpiment, we try not to use this often." That jar bore a warning mark. "An especially strong poison."

"Blues?" I dared to ask.

"Cobalt." He pointed to another jar, also marked with a warning sign. "A mushroom called *turnsole*. Crushed bits of older blue glass. Different oxides. Heat levels. And my secrets."

Inside his jars and on my boards lay sketched sections of Chartres Cathedral's stained glass windows—windows on a grand scale. Some would contain thirty sections and rise over twenty feet in height. Priceless, of course. But for us their cost would greater than we dared imagine.

■

W e were seldom quite alone. Morrisot appeared at odd hours, as if to catch us at some wickedness and he would approach on soundless feet. He had become an unspoken, unofficial sponsor for Gabriel, or so it appeared. A demanding and persistent one.

"Where was that special blue?" He continued to demand. Where was one sample window? Just as men back certain knights in jousts, Morrisot seemed to have his money on Gabriel. But why? Because my glass-maker was the best, I told myself. Simple. Plain. Nothing more than that.

I still relied on Nicolette to warn us of Morrisot's coming but she was not always at hand. Nor could she detect him outside, peering through an open window. When I did, one night, I turned to Gabriel, bent over a table, his hand moving, his eyes intent on work.

I jerked my head toward the window but Gabriel did not look up and Morrisot's face vanished into the night. I wondered if his interest was only in art. Was the older man out to catch us in an act of love? Would he draw twisted pleasure from such a sight? Or was he somehow protecting us, as he had on the quarry's road? The matter was unsettling but I had little time to think.

"Your stepfather's coming." Nicolette thrust her dark head into the room; her eyes flashed a warning. "On his way to start his ovens."

"Well?" Gabriel said. "Of course."

"Of course." Nicolette pouted for him.

I noticed her eyelashes were so long they swept her cheeks. She had left her long hair loose, smooth and sleek; she tossed her head back in a gesture that seemed practiced.

Nicolette knew how to make her hair fall into one long beckoning finger down her back. As Gabriel looked up, she tossed the hair again and smiled at him. I guessed she'd pinched her lips and cheeks to give them a ripe color.

"I look out for you, sir,"she added.

"No need." His gaze stayed on his work.

Her eyes were hard as black stones.

"Indeed," she murmured and withdrew.

I did not like what I saw in her gaze.

Nor did I like Gabriel's absent gaze now. A weed of fear grew within me and like all weeds, it spawned others. Gabriel hardly seemed to notice me ever since Nicolette had burst in upon us. Maybe he no longer needed me; not the way he once had. Were her flirtations beginning to work on him? Was she finally drawing his attention from me?

Perhaps, as with some artists, his wife or mistress was his work. When we had first spoken about love, his artistic efforts were far less consuming. Had I become a nuisance, a distraction?

My greatest dread was this: perhaps his passion for me had faded. Often, his hand would brush mine; our shoulders would touch, but he no longer reached for me. We were so chaste, I worried.

I wondered if he was, in fact, erasing our past from his mind. Many men, I knew, could not stay in love with one woman for long. We were wedded, as I believed—but without a marriage contract. Why had Gabriel not sealed our vows officially? Had he forgotten? Or lost interest?

I kept these thoughts buried deep within me where, as such thoughts do, they festered. The more they did, the more distant I became and the more distant I was, the more distant was he. When I pulled back, he pulled back even further.

Quiet and withdrawn, Gabriel spoke less and less to me. Now he searched for the right parable to make a new window but he did not speak of it or ask my help. I retreated from him into my own protective silence.

Finally, one night, I told him I would not be coming back into the cellar. Neither of us spoke our hearts and that was our greatest failing. We were two sensitive souls, easily wounded, and now the wounding had gone deeper than the knife-grinder's blade.

That night, instead of going to the cellar, I went to the cathedral's ruins, almost cleared of rubble. I thought of my first weeks here with Gabriel. That time seemed as if they belonged to someone else. I must have misread them, I thought. How could I know for certain?

Now, I neared the place where Gabriel and I had met: the South Tower of the cathedral's shell. Something twisted within me. Gathering my skirts, I climbed the spiral stairs.

I remembered how desperate I'd felt on that June night, when he had followed me here. Tonight I came alone, level-headed, with a light, and without footsteps behind me. I had only come here to remember what had been.

At the top step of the spiral staircase, I stepped out into the open belfry, then drew back. A man's silhouette rose before me. I was so startled it took me an instant to see who it was.

Gabriel was waiting there for me.

I stopped short and stared at him. He reached for me with both arms and drew me against him. His mouth pressed mine; no lack of passion now.

Finally, he tipped my head back and kissed down my throat and we were a long time in the tower. Even so, we both seemed afraid to speak and so we descended in an odd strained silence.

"Well?" I said the next day. "You only kiss me at night in the South Tower, is that so?"

"Didn't make that rule, did I?"

I drew a breath and then another.

"I fear I'm just a passing...thing to you."

He turned about and stared at me.

"*My* fear, Cecile—I thought *you'd* cooled."

"You drew back, I thought, so I did, too."

"You did. I did. Both afraid to speak."

I flushed. "And we're so...virtuous."

"Yes. Hate it." He kicked the table. "At night, in bed, how I want you. But I can't put you in danger. I want to protect you, my Cecile."

"From what?" I searched his face. "Who?"

"Spying eyes. Scandal-mongers. Morrisot."

"He's gone—there's nothing to see."

"Doubt he's finished with us yet."

I paced the cellar, watching the ripple of fire on the stone walls. "Of late, the road to you, it's been hard. I felt as if I'd fallen into a ditch and no one would pull me out."

I waited for Gabriel to speak.

He didn't. I went on.

"In that ditch, fears came at me like thieves, stealing all my hopes." I turned my back, ashamed of such plain-spoken words. Gabriel made no reply. There was a long and painful silence. Finally, I turned to look at him, expecting a look back. But no.

He was drawing.

"I'll go." I snapped.

"Stay. Need you."

"Really? How?"

"Just look."

"Where?"

"Here."

"I don't see..."

I glanced about the cellar, looking for a clue in its stone walls, its quiet ovens, its great crouching tables. There was nothing inspirational about this room or anything I'd said.

He beckoned and held me to him, his arm reaching out so fast, I almost went off balance. I lifted the lanthorn higher as he showed me how he'd inscribed his smaller boards.

"They're glorious." I gazed at them. "But... that's not me. It's a man. Wounded, robbed. And here, a man lying in a ditch...."

"You, in a man's guise. See now? It's a story I must design. You told it just now, Cecile. You spoke of being in a ditch and I saw it. Then it came: the story of the Good Samaritan." He was excited, flushed as a boy. "Almost gave up. Couldn't see the figure unless it was you."

His charcoal flew over a fresh board.

"Can art really happen this way?"

"Why not?" He smiled at me.

"Right here?" My eyes swept the rough walls of the room. "In this house? With drafts? With mice? With stone cellars?"

"With *you*. Most important." He hesitated, thinking. "Cecile, you give me another idea. It could make a lovely picture in stained glass."

"What then? Tell me."

"Remember the river?"

"We walked there together."

"Girls dry their wet hair beside it?" Gabriel glanced at my unruly curls. "On hands and knees, you said. Hair flung out before them in the sun?"

"We all did that. An idea waits there?"
"Hate to ask you this. Kneel down?"
"Hair flung out?" I began to guess.
"Just so. A moment. You don't mind?"
"Like this?" Loosening my hair, I knelt.
"Yes." His voice was soft. "Like that."
"You see another woman now, I think."
"Her tears washed her Master's feet."
"She dried them with her long hair."
"Beautiful to me, that story," he said.
"And to me. Mary Magdalene's window."
"Ah, Cecile. This one I draw from life."

Gabriel finished inscribing this design as Nicolette stepped into the room, swinging her hips. My stepfather tramped down and fired up the ovens. Design boards and charcoal were stowed in a cup-board. Work tables were pushed against walls.

Changing my apron, I turned back into Cecile, the baker's daughter. At least for a morning. By night, I had baked many loaves. And in the span of one day, Gabriel had sketched a series of windows.

Later, much later, I studied his inscribed drawings. So deft they were, I marveled: each frame was like a page in great book. Gabriel set a section of the Good Samaritan story inside a quatrefoil, so like a flower centered in four petals, each telling a section of the story.

Mary Magdalene's body formed a graceful curve, her hair flung out, as she bent to dry the feet of Jesus. And there was Adam and Eve. Well. There was Adam. Eve's figure was hardly formed. I watched him draw each sketch into his copybook and then, in our dusty cellar, he took a breath.

"I must ask you to be my Eve," he said.

"The way I posed with the scales?"

"But without the scales."

"Of course, without the scales."

"Without your tunic."

"In my chemise?"

He nodded. "Nothing lewd."

"It's a risk," I said at last.

He nodded. "Will you take it?"

■

Posing as Eve nearly cost me my life.

There was nothing to warn us of danger: no omen, no sign, no sudden foreboding or apprehension. It seemed so very simple, even safe, there at the start. To avoid any chance of discovery, my aunt let us use her cellar as a work room for an afternoon.

There we would be guarded as we went about the design of a new sample window. Our methods would be thought unseemly, even scandalous, by anyone except my aunt. In fact, I think she more than a little pleased to take part in our scheme.

We came to her apothecary's shop at slightly different times, by somewhat different routes. My aunt hustled each of us down the steep steps leading to her cellar.

Its walls were stone and the place was crowded, chill and damp, even in summer. There was a smell of mice and mold. Hardly the Garden of

Eden, Gabriel remarked as he ducked hanging herbs and strings of onions that dangled above his head, grazing it from time to time.

He watched as I peeled my long tunic off. Through my ankle-length chemise, backlit by a lanthorn, I knew the outlines of my body showed. Gabriel watched that outline as an artist and, I noticed, he watched as a man.

In the silence we could hear the clack of footsteps above in the shop and the slow drip-drip of water from somewhere nearby. I stood with my hands at my sides. He wasn't drawing.

"Cecile, I must ask," he said at last.

"Of course." I faked serenity.

"Take off more for me?"

I hesitated. "What would that be?"

"Your shoes and stockings."

"My what?" I stared at him.

"I don't think Eve wore shoes."

For a moment we both had to stifle giddy laughter. Every time I tried to stop, I started once more and then he would catch it. Nervous laughter, this was, as we heard the shop's bells chime above us and the cellar's rodents skitter about. On this day, of all days, it happened that my aunt's shop was busier than usual—as were the mice.

"I need one pose," Gabriel whispered..

"Ready, then." I quelled a shiver.

He lay a wooden chopping block across his knees. This small board, already prepared, would serve. Out came his sharpest tools. The scrape of them seemed loud in that cellar space, with its silent crowd of barrels.

I looked about at baskets, chests and stores of dried foodstuffs. The light was dim. Gabriel had placed an oil lamp to his right and to his left and there was one behind me. That was all.

I took off my shoes and set them neatly with my clothes, out of the way. There I stood then, in my flimsy linen shift; it grazed the floor. Above, the shop's bells chimed again. More footsteps above.

Facing him, I stood still.

"Turn now. Half-profile."

"Is this right?" I whispered back.

"Just so. I'll be quick, you're cold."

Overhead, footsteps moved toward the door to the cellar stairs. "Not that way, M'sieur," my aunt's voice was sharp. "This way out, thank you, good. *Bon, merci.*" The shop's bells chimed as that customer went off into the street. I let out my breath.

Now there was silence.

Gabriel's strokes seemed loud as he drew me; I could feel my feet grow cold, my neck turn stiff. Something scurried by my heel. I jumped, then took up my pose again . My skin felt cool, my face felt hot.

I watched the artist in the man come out and cock his head one moment, then squint from another angle. He looked down at his board from time to time at his board but his hand moved while he watched my body. I tried to keep still.

"Breathe, M'amselle," He whispered.

"As you wish, M'sieur." I laughed.

He set another lamp before me and, smiling, satisfied, went back to his work. I wondered if he could hear the thudding of my heart; it seemed a huge sound in that space.

So keen was he, so intense, I wondered if he felt as thrilled and aroused as I did. As I turned before the light, I knew my breasts were outlined and, stealing a look, I saw the man within the artist, stealing a look himself.

"Good," he said. "Can you turn?"

"Like so?" I moved with care.

"Stay just as you are."

I froze in place when I heard the shop's bell ring again and more footsteps tapped across the floor above. How much danger might we bring down on my aunt? Surely, she would keep herself safe as she guarded us, or so I devoutly hoped.

I arched my back and flexed my shoulders for an instant, as if to shrug off my fretfulness. My breasts moved underneath my shift. Gabriel cleared his throat and began again on a new board.

"You...have no idea...how hard...this is." He spoke like a tailor with pins in his mouth.

"But I do, believe me," I whispered back.

There was a rustle behind me in the cellar, then a long whisking sound. My glazier's hand paused just above the board. I dared to turn my head and saw my aunt's white cat streak by. Gabriel's hand began to move again and I began once more to breathe.

Above, the shop seemed empty. My aunt's steps reached the cellar door, where she stood sentry. The cellar felt safe and still; all that moved was his hand and our huge shadows, thrown against the cellar's pale stone. I was so entranced, I forgot about my common inner caution: For me, a sense of safety sometimes signals new disaster.

This one came quickly. The cat streaked past me again, jostling the oil lamp and, before I could move, it fell against the hem of my shift.

One finger of flame reached up to catch the hem of my long shift. Paralyzed, I stared at it. I smelled burning cloth and felt heat on my legs. I was too shocked to scream.

Was I about to become a human candle? I gazed at the flame and the suddenly the Great Fire flared before my eyes once more. I saw the cathedral's tapers, my flaming sleeve...then a pulsing blackness. I was falling through the dark.

When I opened my eyes I did not know where I was. There was a mattress beneath me but it wasn't mine. The ceiling was dark wood and did not look readily.

Shafts of light entered the room from several open windows and the light was long and low and amber. Someone held my hand; a priest, come to give me the Last Rites? But there was no priest.

I heard Gabriel's voice.

"Coming around...I think."

"Thank God." My aunt's words.

"Thank God," Gabriel echoed.

I turned my head and looked at her; I realized I was in her bed, where I had often slept as a child. *What soft enamoring of sleep hath you in some soft way...?* She used to sing that to me here, I remembered. I turned my head the other way and saw Gabriel. His hand gripped mine; his rain-gray gaze was pained and tender.

"What...who...the fire?" All the words I ever knew seemed scrambled in my head and I could not quite put them together.

"Fire's out. You're safe, Cecile" But his voice was not quite steady. "My fault, all my fault."

I sat up; the room circled around me.

"We have to finish Eve." I tried to rise.

"No." Gabriel was stern. "Lie back."

"Slowly, slowly now." My aunt fed me almond milk and honey. "We're blessed."

"No real burns, just a scorch." Gabriel smoothed my hair. "You scared me to death."

We had come here just after the noon Angelus bells had rung and now it was late afternoon; the tawny light told the time.

"But the sketch—it's not finished."

"Another time." Gabriel sounded firm.

If there is another time, I thought.

But how likely was that?

■

The damning sketch lay across the Bishop's desk. Rendered with charcoal on paper, the drawing held His Excellency's gaze. That room was still as snow. Then came the accusations: sudden, startling, serious.

All work on the windows must wait until a new matter was resolved. We stood together, Gabriel and I, knee-deep in silence. A breeze fluttered into the room, touched the art, and backed away. Even a breeze would not linger there.

I could hear the grains of sand passing through the hourglass on the Bishop's vast mahogany desk; it seemed immense, a desert space to cross. But I was not to cross it now.

The chamber loomed above us, large and dim, paneled in wood. Its ceiling's beams appeared ready to fall on us. Against one wall, I saw a carved chest, a dark large crouching thing like an animal, poised to spring. Beside us stood a high, forbidding bench.

An hour earlier, the Bishop's summons was delivered by a sweating red-faced lad who stammered at the bakery door. From the shaking of his hands, I knew some new calamity had happened.

As I said, luck always runs out. Everything had gone too smoothly for too long. But after Gabriel's shed was invaded we were always on our guard, even against the clergy and the monks.

I found it hard to admit there could be envy, malice, even violence in such a hallowed endeavor. A human endeavor nonetheless, Gabriel reminded me.

It was a late summer afternoon. The light was slanting through the miles of cornfields, turning them the color of apricots. Around us, the town's ginger-colored roofs seemed the stuff of children's bedtime tales.

To look at Chartres now was to look at a faraway world where supper is laid and lamps are lit and food is blessed and sleep is serene. As we stood before the Bishop, I wondered if such quiet, common evenings would be ours again.

Now I peered over at that drawing on the Bishop's desk. The sketch was not Gabriel's style, I well knew, nor was it his work. And I was surely not the model, posing naked, legs spread wide apart, one hand fondling a breast.

That was the truth of it—but I knew the truth might not matter at all. What the Bishop thought was all that mattered. Someone, then, must wish us ill badly enough to take such a daring and devious risk, just to land us deep in trouble.

The Bishop had finished reading off his list of accusations. Morrisot, behind me, coughed. Near the door, huddled on a stool, my stepfather wept openly. The Bishop went on studying the drawing.

"Who did it?" Gabriel finally demanded.

"You did,"the Bishop snapped. "You, sir."

"Not I. Who is my accuser?"

"He has a right to know." Morrisot spoke.

"I do indeed." Gabriel's voice rose.

The Bishop sighed—an autumn wind in a tall tree. Clearly, he had never thought his plans would come to this: a messy matter spreading like a stain, not easily or neatly resolved. I turned toward Morrisot but he slipped out of the study.

The Bishop seemed intent on studying his hands. I glanced sideways at Gabriel while we waited; the muscles in his jaw were working as they had when I'd brought him this news, this summons. Since that moment, everything had changed.

"Outrageous," Gabriel had shouted.

"Yes. But the Bishop thinks not."

"Your reputation....Ruined."

"It's *your* reputation that's important."

"You're in more danger. I put you there."

"You did no wrong, *we* did no wrong."

"Terrible irony, that." A ghost of a smile had played about his lips. "If I must suffer this, I might as well suffer for what I wanted."

"What was that?" I whispered.

"For you. You knew that, Cecile?"

My stepfather had plunged into the room then and our private time vanished like so much steam from a crock of pottage.

When the baker listened to the news, he had paced the floor, repeatedly slamming his fist into hand as he often did when in distress. I waited. And then my stepfather had rounded on me.

"I knew it, I feared it. How could you do this to me?" He had shouted. "How could you, girl?"

"I didn't, Papa, we did nothing."

"Nothing, Sir." Gabriel repeated.

There was a small defeated silence.

"It doesn't matter if you did or if you didn't." My stepfather said at last. "They think you did and that's the only thing that matters. It's over. All of it, over and done with now."

And then, for the first time since my mother's death, I heard my stepfather sob—a raucous noise, like the sound of strong cloth tearing, harder it was to bear than the silence.

I went to Henri Dufort but he jerked away and stomped off to a corner. Even if we followed him and talked to him, I knew that he would not believe a word of our denials. Would anyone?

Slowly, quietly, we had closed the shutters of the shop. We had banked the fires. I had cleared the table. The room sank into dimness.

The place seemed caught, perhaps forever, in a winter's dusk. We had moved slowly and deliberately, like people readying a chamber for a wake.

And then we'd gone upstairs into Gabriel's room, as it was now—that spare space, fit for the monk he once thought to be: the simple bed, the stool. My marriage chest. The light pooling on the floor.

We had sat beside each other for some time, my head against his shoulder and then we held each other—gently at first, then fiercely, furiously, as if a wind blew all around us and we were clinging to each other for our lives.

We could not know if or when we would have time together again. I felt warmth creeping into me, like blood, like breath within my chest; I had not realized I'd grown so cold.

How long we'd held each other I don't know, nor did it matter. If not for those minutes together, I don't know how we would have endured the inquisition in the Bishop's study, an hour later.

An hour later, there we were, all of us standing side by side. I looked at Morrisot, wondering if some aid lay with him, but he did not meet my eyes.

Instead he slipped out of the chamber through one of its side doors. Perhaps he had gone to get some notes, some journal he had kept, some confession he might then force us to sign.

But when at last he did return, his long thin hands were empty and his face was gaunt. He stepped into the room as one steps carefully into a marsh. He turned his head and as he did, Morrisot murmured to someone unseen; someone waiting in the passageway behind him. ∎

I thought to see someone like Abbot Chevan appear. But it was Nicolette who came through the doorway. She did not look at us, only at the Bishop and at Morrisot. An odd smile curled about her mouth and turned her dark eyes almost serpentine: a look I had seen in them before.

As she came in, I was pleased to see her: cohort, confidante, housekeeper, friend, she would surely be an ally. I thought our trusted Nicolette had been called in our defense. And so I waited for our accuser; the appearance of a neighbor, a priest, or even the cathedral's sexton.

Nicolette lifted her chin and speared me with one defiant glance. And then, with a shock, I knew. I felt the way I did, as a child, when my stepbrother had pushed me from behind to make me fall.

"Under ordinary circumstances," the Bishop was saying now. "We would question such grave accusations. These circumstances, I fear, are far from ordinary. We must trust the most reliable and likely source of private information."

He glanced around the room before going on. "M'amselle Nicolette has a distinguished lineage. I knew her father well. She is gentry, one of us, but also an intimate of the Duforts for three years."

Nicolette smiled at him and at Morrisot.

"Her fine family came to grief, as you know, hence her employment. And..." his finger tapped the drawing. "...she has brought us vital tidings. An act of courage, I believe. Irrefutable evidence."

"*Irrefutable?*" Gabriel's voice was cutting. "I demand to see this so-called drawing."

Morrisot nodded at the Bishop. Gabriel faced his accusers. The damning sketch was passed across the Bishop's desk, transported by a page across the study, and placed like a silver tray in my glazier's outstretched hands.

As he scanned the sketch, Gabriel's face went taut with restrained fury; for a moment I thought I might tear the drawing to pieces. Then, passing the sketch back, he confronted the Bishop, his assistant, and Morrisot.

"*Not* my work." Gabriel's tone was stinging. "Dare you accuse me? Not only of poor workmanship but outright fraud?"

"Nicolette?" The Bishop rose in all his purples from his chair. The room seemed to contract around us and a bee droned at the window. "You still say this is the Master's work? You still say your Mistress let him draw her totally naked in this lewd pose?"

"I do, Your Excellency."

Her perfectly starched wimple covered her glorious charcoal hair so she could look the humble girl, I guessed, but I recalled her toss that hair before Gabriel in the light.

Somewhere, underneath that cap, her hair was tossing still. Her chin lifted; her lips curved. A bone-white collar covered the creamy cleavage she had let Gabriel see when we were last together.

I remembered his brusqueness with her and that flash of something dangerous in her dark eyes, now carefully lowered. Nicolette had formed a shell of purity about herself for this occasion; the demure and docile look of a shepherdess, seen from afar. Truly, she had dressed to play this part.

All her boldness was concealed like a flagon wrapped in cotton wool. How sure she was of herself; sure enough to toss another glance at us. And that glance was not lost on Morrisot. I watched him watching her quite carefully as she moved and smiled and spoke.

"Nic, you can't mean this." I wanted to shout; I wanted to shake her hard. "Tell me you don't."

She had been like a sister to me for so long, I had not feared the danger signs, the envy that was always waiting within her. She often teased me for trusting others too easily. Indeed, I thought now.

Once or twice I'd invited Nicolette her to borrow my clothes. I recalled her talk of silks she and her mother used to own. I had not paid attention to the look on her face; not then, not other times, when we spoke of her lost luxuries from the distant past.

Nor had I feared her wildness or her anger, even in her outbursts at vendors in the marketplace when food was not quite fresh. No tantrums from her now, however. Not here, not today.

She was perfectly controlled, it seemed, in command of herself and, in fact, the men in the study. Nicolette ignored me, speaking to the Bishop, his assistant, and to Morrisot as if I were not there.

"I have seen more, far more than I have told, yes, I can tell you many other things." She skimmed her words like stones across still water. "I feared it was not seemly to speak about such matters. I have let the drawing speak for me."

Nicolette's speeches sounded practiced, as if she had refined them a great many times in front of a looking glass or a shop's window pane. Here was a prepared performance, almost overdone, I thought. Had Morrisot, that shrewd man, noticed what I saw?

It seemed the Bishop had not. She had read him well and taken the good man in. Clever girl, she had played on her family's connections and her father's friendship with men of importance.

Gentry. Came to grief. And who were we? Only bakers, however prosperous. Only an artist, however well-known. His Excellency scanned our faces, one by one. His gaze fixed on Gabriel.

"I remind you," the Bishop spoke again. "This sketch was made on *your* paper, rendered with *your* charcoal. Of late, you were designing the Adam and Eve window. How ironic, Sir."

His Excellency looked about his study to emphasize that irony. "It seems our artist has found his Eve. He and Cecile have worked in close proximity for weeks, at my behest." The Bishop's voice sharpened. "My trust has been abused."

"Nicolette." I turned on her. "If you know who did this, why not tell us now? A friend, a secret suitor, who? Of all people, how could you let someone do this? Would you be so ungrateful?"

"Ungrateful?" She gave one of her practiced, dimpled smile, although her eyes were hard and cold.

"You seek to ruin Gabriel—and me?"

"I must do the right thing, no?" She looked down with piety. "Do the right thing or damn my soul with my own silence?"

She looked down at her graceful hands.

"I did not wish to come forward. But my mother, rest her soul, taught me well." Nicolette threw the Bishop a pleading look. "I learned right from wrong when Mama was the mistress of our own house. I came to the Duforts as an orphan who lost everything. I trusted them. But I must speak true."

Another string of prepared words. Nicolette was superb; she was heart-rending. And she played so well to the Bishop's sensibilities. Nicolette had made herself seem pitiful, the troubadour's version of damsel in distress.

The Bishop, as I have said, was kind. He saw before him a hapless lady, coming forward on the side of truth and righteousness—she appeared as Fortune's victim. The daughter of an old friend, this maiden, Nicolette needed to be rescued.

"Of course she must 'speak true.'" The Bishop turned an icy gaze on us. "What motive could she have for fraud? For lying?"

"Envy." I tried to keep my voice from shaking. "Envy long held in. Envy on several counts."

"*Envy?*" my stepfather roared. "Why the hell would she envy us?....Begging Your Excellency's pardon, damn it. I mean...." He fell silent.

I could not answer without speaking of all Gabriel had together. Nicolette must have spied upon us and seen far too much. How we had trusted her; at least, I had. If pressed, she might have far more to reveal about us.

Always flirtatious, always after an important man, Nicolette had first wanted Bonnet. Since his death, she had wanted Gabriel. Her pride in her family roots had made her feel it was her right to have him, too; her right over mine.

But how was I to speak so, without giving too much away? Gabriel must have wondered the same thing. We said nothing, searching for the right words, and that was a grave mistake. We waited too long; our silence damned us.

"You have no answer, I see. Such silence itself speaks most eloquently." The Bishop sharp glance raked our faces. "Needless to say, this is a matter of importance and further consideration.

Another stretched silence.

"Nicolette has more to say," he went on, "Perhaps others will come forth to speak as well. Meanwhile, Cecile is remanded to her father's keeping and you, sir— "He looked directly at Gabriel. "You will stay in *my* house until the Chapter meets. Meanwhile, all glass design and glass-making remains halted."

The Bishop's ring came down on his desk.

∎

I heard that sound long after I had left the Bishop's palace; long after my stepfather had steered me home with one heavy hand on my shoulder and the other and gripping mine, as if I might bolt. I expected a beating but got none.

The house was unnaturally still, except when the bakery bell rang and I pretended all was well. I ran between the shop and my stepfather, hoping to rouse him. The man just sat in a sodden silence and drank the afternoon and evening away.

I paced.

I prayed.

I thought a thousand flickering thoughts.

At twilight, I knew what I must do. If only I had the courage and nerve to take such a risk.

My aunt had come to visit before dusk; she'd a sense of trouble near me, I knew, though her excuse for the visit was to fetch extra bread. How had she known I needed something far more precious—her advice? I drew her up into the solar and there, I told her everything. She listened in that way she had, her head to one side, her eyes never leaving my face.

I could not help but notice her threadbare clothes, her worn tunic and neatly mended sleeves. Her shoes were worn down, too, I saw. Even so, she was still elegant, my aunt, and there was wisdom and experience in her eyes.

This woman, I thought, could look to be an abbess or a queen, even now. Practical and mystical, she always said her knowledge came from prayer. Her own life, both rich and poor, gave her insight into the inner workings of Nicolette.

"She will not repent or change her story," my aunt said at last. "Her spirit will never bend."

"What can I do? The Bishop believes her."

"The bold thing." My aunt pressed her fingertips together. "Yes. Only a bold stroke will do what is needed now."

"How bold?" I felt like bird trying to fly.

"You must overturn this quickly, my child, before Nicolette reveals all she knows."

"And what of my Gabriel? His disgrace?"

"You said, 'your Gabriel.' You love this man?"

Nodding, I felt tears sting my eyes.

"So I thought." My aunt sighed. "And he loves you. I see this love in him. Almost too much."

"You do?" I felt just a bit lighter.

"Cecile, it is you who must rescue him, I think. He will withdraw into himself, he won't speak out, that's not his way." My aunt shook her head. "He will quit the competition if you do not act now."

"His voice is more respected."

"*You must speak*, Cecile. But mark me well, when you do, you will draw attention to yourself. The Bishop admires courage and he will admire you. This may change his opposition to Morrisot's marriage suit for you—his brother's wish, *cherie.*"

"Then I will not speak." I set out each word like bits of cloth. "I can't risk that. To marry Morrisot and not Gabriel—that would be death for me."

"But can you let Gabriel be disgraced? And yourself? And your family?"

The floor seemed to melt away.

"No," I said at last. "I can't."

"Perhaps the matter will come out a different way, only freeing you and him for each other. I will pray hard and long, be certain of that."

"Please God, may it be so."

"Use Morrisot." Her eyes glinted now. "He is the key, I think. Powerful, yes, but he can be used."

"I can't go out to see him."

"You'll draw him here, Cecile."

"I don't know how."

My aunt covered my hands with hers; they were warm and firm and I could feel each delicate bone. "You will know how," she said then. "But don't wait, do this thing tonight."

My aunt's brown eyes were kind and canny and concerned. "This sort of love you have brings joy—and sometimes pain." She looked away. "Your first task is protection, even at high risk."

She blew the hair off my forehead and I caught a whiff of her familiar smell: autumn, apples, cloves and honey. It was as if she blew some courage into me, and life, and hope.

I wanted to cling to her; I let her go instead. I watched her regal figure disappearing up the street and after she had gone, I knew I must begin to plan and plan as boldly as I could.

Unobserved, I must move throughout the house. This had never been difficult before but now I had to guard myself against Nicolette. I didn't know how she had the nerve to return to our house, but here she was: flushed and delighted with her triumphant interview.

In her own mind, I was sure, she was mistress of this household now. At supper, she did not serve but sat at the table with us and all the while, my mind was spinning, spinning, spinning.

My stepfather spoke not a word, continuing to drink himself into a stupor—much to my purposes. He would sleep hard and long.

And Nicolette? She would not sleep at all, I thought; she would plan and scheme and dream of her new life. And she would set her sights on new prospects, new men: perhaps even Morrisot: just the one to make her a lady again.

That prize might have an extra savor for her, I believe, because she knew he had proposed to me. The chilly, lonely, bereaved widower, with pretty

Nicolette upon his arm: what a perfect sight—one I would love to see.

I watched the rush-lamps throwing light against the walls. I watched my stepfather's head sink lower toward his cup of ale. Above all, I kept a careful watch on Nicolette.

Her gaze was faraway but when I spoke, her eyes lit on me like a bird on a branch. She had taken off her maid's wimple and cast it aside. Like two black streams, her hair framed her face.

I had seen her study her reflection in her bowl of broth and in the blade of a broad knife; she knew how beautiful she looked, indeed. This kind of victory was becoming to her.

Now, while she was reveling in it, a bit drunk on her own powers—now was the time to send her out. I wagered she could be tempted to go off on a certain kind of errand and my wager proved correct.

"Nicolette, I wish..." I paused.

"You wish me dead." A bitter laugh.

"I wish to make a confession," I went on, ignoring her. "A confession to M'sieur Morrisot. Before I see the Bishop."

"To Morrisot." She was not prepared for this. "A confession, you say? Why not to a priest?"

"The Bishop is a priest. But first Morrisot, I need his counsel." I gambled then. "That's the only way you'll get any admission out of me."

Her eyes narrowed. For the first time, I saw an odd look there, the look of someone who could lose control, and that look disturbed me.

She was an actor of great skill, I realized; all those years, feigning friendship, coveting what I had here. But she was not acting now; she was intrigued and interested. "A confession," she repeated.

"Yes, Nic. He must know my mind before I tell the Bishop. It's only fair. But you know I can't go to him. I'm confined to this house, at the Bishop's command." I tried to thread a tremor through my voice. I felt like Nic, a betrayer, a deceiver, but what I said next was true enough: "I must speak, here, tonight, before I lose hold of my courage."

"I can bring him here for you." I watched her smooth her hair and flush again with pleasure. "He will come with me, if I ask him, oh yes, I am sure."

She left her wimple off when she went out.

While she was gone, I searched the house and found all I needed. Whatever happened to me, I would not let Gabriel be humiliated or destroyed.

That much I knew. That much was decided. I had moved nothing in the house. The place would have its own say, if it had the chance, tonight. I wondered what Gabriel was doing now?

Pacing, no doubt. Planning for us both to run away, perhaps. Wondering what I was wondering. I could feel his strength flow toward me like a river's current. With that I could face Morrisot's arrival.

In a short while, Nicolette had done her work and done it well indeed. She must have been convincing; few could resist Nicolette, I knew, and here was the proof.

The man I awaited was here. ■

B reathless in the heat, Morrisot stooped through the doorway. He looked to me, as always, like a bare-branched winter tree. There was harshness in this man—so I had heard, at least about his business dealings. But there was wisdom in him as well. Would he not want a neat way out of this tangle?

I believed he would, else he would lose his own hopes for those incomparable windows he wished to sponsor. The windows and perhaps a bride. *Gets what he wants, that one,* Nicolette herself had said. I guessed which way he wanted this matter to fall out.

"Cecile, you let me down."

"M'sieur Morrisot, you don't know all."

The opening steps in this risky dance.

"If I could confess to you in some private place." A curtsy, of sorts: the second step in the dance. "A place where we cannot be overheard."

"If you must, show me the way."

The dance led down the stairs to my cellar pastry room and the wooden boards inscribed with Gabriel's designs. The room had always looked spacious before; not tonight.

Now it appeared too small, too bright with lamplight, confining as a cupboard. But nearby were those inscribed boards and tables and they would speak for me. They would speak for us.

"This is how the M'sieur Larue does it, inscribes his designs on wooden boards, on tabletops." Morrisot was pleased to learn a secret. "I've heard of this from other glass-makers, of course, but never seen it close." The man looked up at me. "What is this white surface he works upon?"

"He used to work with chalked boards." I tried to keep my voice low and even. Panic would be disastrous. I thought of my aunt. *Use Morrisot, he is the key.* I thought of Gabriel, pacing, sending his strength to me, as he did the night he called me down from the South Tower. I regained my balance.

"And now?" Morrisot touched a board.

"No more chalk, he finds it easiest to inscribe each new design into a flour paste I make for him. Surprising that great windows rise from bakers' table, but so it is. Nicolette could not make such designs in flour on such boards. She lacks the skill, the knowledge—*and* the tools."

"But that lewd drawing was done on paper." Morrisot looked hard at me. "*Gabriel's* paper, M'amselle Cecile."

"Indeed. M'sieur Larue rarely uses paper. It's too hard to get, too costly for a sketch. If he used it at all, he would keep it for a finished project. His paper is in short supply. Two or three sheets. Nor does he keep it hidden. Anyone could steal it."

Morrisot gave me a penetrating look.

Above our heads, I heard Nicolette's restless footsteps on the entry's floor. I had to give her credit for fooling a man like Morrisot. Unless this was his own elaborate web.

"When each design is finished," I went on, "the Glass Master draws it small and sets it into his copybook. You looked at it, and the designs held there, Sir, over our dinner. If you search that copybook, you will not find that lewd drawing; indeed, any lewd drawing."

I swallowed a thread of desperation in my voice. "M'sieur Larue does not leave loose sketches lying about, he records each carefully. Ask him. Try him."

"And so, you say, that damning sketch would not issue from Larue's hand." Morrisot's voice was hard and formal: the voice of a king and council all at once. "Or so you maintain."

"I do." My voice had the chime of truth. "Nor would he leave his work about, where anyone and everyone could see it."

"Nicolette vows she found it hidden in his room. In a chest, she says, while she put away his freshly laundered clothes."

"Impossible. That room holds the marriage chest for my own small trousseau. Our guest keeps no clothing there. Indeed he could not, since I have the chest's only key." I held it up before me; it felt cold and solid in my hand. "Try it if you like."

Morrisot turned to me, his eyes cautious. "Do not think to lie to me, Cecile Dufort. I'll find you out, you know. I always win in the end."

"I only think to ask your help," I murmured.

"And what help do you imagine?" His tone was stiff as ever, his gaze holding me. I met that gaze directly and mine did not waver. His eyes changed then: I saw cunning, control, and a glimmer of kindness, like a light beneath a firmly bolted door.

"M'sieur Morrisot." I kept my voice strong and even. "Make this right. Only a man like you can do that. I don't know how to convince the Bishop. You know how better than I. And if you searched this house, you would find that Nicolette did far more than a housekeeper's work."

"Why would she wish to do so?" His voice tightened. The room seemed close and hot. From somewhere upstairs I heard her footsteps tap across the floor, back and forth, back and forth.

"Envy," I was firm. "As I told the Bishop, Envy and spite." Nicolette's family is not of the servant class and she has waited years to change her station. This is her chance to win a man like you. Perhaps you're the prize she hoped to win." I took a breath, "She has hatred, now, for M'sieur Gabriel. He turned from her flirtations."

"Because he is in love with you." Morrisot's tone commanded me to look at him. "And that love has grown, reflected in his art?"

"I cannot say." No show of feelings now. "But I say, upon my life, this business could do a great wrong. It might destroy the Master Glazier and his windows—those windows you so desire." I drew a breath. "Not to mention what would become of me. You alone can convince your brother, His Excellency. I know your sense of honor. And his."

"You have my attention, Cecile."

I paused and took my last bold chance. "If you do not act, Sir, you will never know if Nicolette won her game with you and the Bishop. You both strike me as men who would not wish to be tricked."

Morrisot measured me with his eyes and seemed to listen, to my words as if they still hung in the air. And then, for the first time, I saw his face change. The flinty control was gone. His color rose. His jaw tightened. His hands curled into fists.

He was starting to see another plan, unthinkable before: A desperate and daring housemaid playing with Morrisot and his brother, making lordly fools of them. Such men would not permit themselves to be outdone or outwitted by anyone. And by a servant girl? Intolerable. But not impossible.

"Sir," I prompted him. "Search the house."

Without a word, Morrisot moved up the stairs. He strode across the entryway and into the solar. There he cast his eyes about but found nothing out of place, nothing revealing. He lit a lamp and looked about him twice.

Unconvinced, slightly breathless, he climbed the next flight of stairs to the bed chambers. So angry was he, the air in the house was disturbed, as by a sudden wind. His whippet's eyes missed nothing: the charcoal sticks in Gabriel's room; my locked marriage chest and my single key.

I followed as quickly as I could and Nicolette was right behind me, a glint of fear in her eyes as she dashed up toward her sleeping place. Morrisot was faster than she and he blocked the doorway with his tree-like frame.

"No one is to come in here," he hissed and we drew back. He had gathered his power around him like a cloak and entered the chamber. There, with one swift stroke, Morrisot, breathing hard, turned Nicolette's pallet upside down and inside out. Nothing. Nothing yet.

Then he neared Nicolette's rosewood chest from her old home—and that was when I heard her gasp. Morrisot threw open the chest as Nicolette protested: This was nothing, she insisted. A storage chest, no more.

Even so, when Morrisot demanded she produce her keys, she had to open her right hand. He snatched them from her. Trying one key, then others, he found the one he wanted. He threw open the chest and tossed clothing on the floor. The man's eyes lit.

From the bottom of the chest he drew out three sticks of charcoal, a knife to sharpen them, and one remaining piece of paper. Stooping under the sloped roof, Morrisot ordered me to hold up his lamp.

In its light he studied what he held with care in both hands. His eyes narrowed; his gaze grew intense. I strained for a glimpse of what he saw before him, spread out like a map.

It was indeed a map, of sorts. A map of a well-endowed nude woman. A practice sketch, I supposed, one preceding the next one: that damning picture centered on the Bishop's broad desk.

This drawing was awkward, out of proportion, with visible smudges and twice drawn lines. The woman pictured there had a familiar face and figure: the long dark hair, the full breasts, the long-lashed eyes, the thighs spread apart.

"Nicolette Marchand." Morrisot reached for her as she made to dart away from him, from us, no doubt from the house itself. The man's rage lent him strength; Nic was not quite swift enough or strong enough to break free of him. Not then, not later.

~~~

Later, in front of the Bishop's massive desk, the we all stood stiffly in the chamber as we had before. I wanted to give some sign to Gabriel, who managed a discreet smile at me. He looked as if he'd had little sleep, if any. All I could do was return his smile with equal discretion.

Dusk's purples were darkening the windows but dozens of candles blazed from sconces on the walls. Above our heads, a candle-beam had also been lit and its flames rippled above us. Light played over every face and glinted from the Bishop's ring.

The study smelled of beeswax and leather and wood. Again the desk seemed too vast a space to cross. But now we had a chance, however small. This affair would have to play out as God would have it. Not for the first time that day, I prayed.

We were ranged about the room in the same order: Gabriel beside me, Nicolette with Morrisot, the Bishop, alone in his purples, seated at the desk with his assistant, Father Louis, at his side. As Morrisot told his story, I watched the room fading in and out. I had eaten nothing today. *No fainting*, I told myself. *No matter what.*

Nicolette watched everyone. I saw her eyes search Morrisot's thin face, and the Bishop's fuller one, and Father Louis's fleshy one—and the evidence before them. Then she glanced over her shoulder toward the door. I could almost see the thoughts streaking through her mind: her choices, her decisions, her plans shifting like water..

"Is this your work?" The Bishop gave Gabriel the newly discovered drawing from our house.

There was a dense silence as my glazier took the damning paper in his hands. "Fraud. Again." His voice was like the frozen surface of a pond. "Bad art as well. If I claimed such drawings, Your Excellency, you would not want my windows."

"Deceived." The color of the Bishop's face passed from red to purple. "I pitied the girl, God help me. She took me for a fool. And my brother."

"Your Excellency, I did not." Nicolette was grabbing at any string. "I see in you a man of wisdom and a man of mercy and forgiveness and—"

"No flattery," Morrisot snapped. "There's been too much of that already. It won't do now."

"This is an affront to you." Gabriel looked about. "And to me and to M'amselle Dufort."

For the first and last time, I heard the Bishop utter an apology and I stood in admiration as I saw the strength in his humility. This man had made an extraordinary statement and we acknowledged it with gratitude, Gabriel and I.

Nicolette's chest was heaving but she said no more. While everyone stood gazing at the Bishop, she made a small noise in her throat and, wild-eyed, trembling, she bolted from the room.

"Let her go," Morrisot advised. "Too cunning to stay here, she'll be gone come morning. And I give thanks for that. If we take any action now—and I wager she knows this—it would only disgrace us and the town and the cathedral."

For a moment, the chamber was silent. We could hear the hissing of the candle wicks and the drip of wax. Through an open casement, a faint breeze blew into the room and this time, it remained.

"M'amselle Cecile deserves our thanks." Gabriel could not keep himself from saying that. "She dared to speak. She put things right."

"My thanks, sir, but I give our Bishop credit." I meant that. I forced myself to add Morrisot's name. Best to stay in both men's good graces.

The Bishop's brother cast Gabriel a sharp look and we both saw it. For now we put it from our minds. There was nothing further he or anyone could do to us tonight.

"Indeed, our thanks to you, M'amselle." The Bishop looked at me. "Your are excused, free to go home and move about, as you are, M'sieur." The Bishop stood. "We all must pledge to keep this sordid business to ourselves. That is agreed?"

I nodded and bobbed another curtsy, just for good measure; I could breathe again. Now that this was over, my legs felt like straws. All I wanted was to be gone from there and at home with Gabriel.

As always, he and I would walk there by different lanes, Gabriel first, as I preferred. I would tell my stepfather what happened in the morning; he had drunk himself to sleep by now, I knew. Tonight, Gabriel and I would have some freedom in the house.

Now, farewells were over. I lingered for a moment in the palace's entry, allowing a short time to pass. And then I was out into the darkness, feeling free and reckless and redeemed.

The town unreeled below me as if I had never seen its terraced streets before: the narrow houses, the thread-like lanes. I walked on. So great was my relief, I did not glance behind me.

■

Halfway home, I felt two hands grab me by the hair, jerk me off my feet and throttle me about the neck.

At first this seemed a fragment of the darkness flying at me like a shard of shattered crockery. I had not heard Nicolette creeping near until she was upon me. Her hair, her scent, for form were clear to me then. I knew who she was before I saw her in the full moon's light.

I should have guessed. This proud girl was not one to go quietly. I pulled away and stood up with the force that comes only from fury. She took me by the shoulders, shaking me and hissing in my ear, "*Whore.* You're Gabriel's whore, we both know it."

"Let go, don't be a fool." Struggling to breathe, I kicked her knees. "Stop before I hurt you."

"Hurt *me*? That you have, Cecile. You charmed them all and ruined my best plans." She spat the words and held me off. "You undid me with your own deceptions—twice."

"I told the truth." Dodging, darting, I ducked under her arm and swung around, pinning her hands behind her back. I did not want to wake the neighborhood but I was far too angry to keep still.

"You undid yourself, Nic."

"He should have been mine."

"Would he want a traitor?"

"You, Cecile? Calling names?"

"Shut up. Or wake the *bâilli*."

The dark seemed jagged now, pieces of the town jumping and jerking before my eyes as Nicolette broke free and pulled my face close to hers. Grappling with each other we rolled and struggled in the street as the town slept on.

"Whore," she spat again. "That's what I must become now—turned out, sent away in shame to Paris. What choice do you leave me, Cecile? You and your precious artist?"

"Listen, Nicolette. This was your choice, the whole of it. Your scheme, your gamble."

"Bitch." She raked my arm with her nails. "You kept me from my rightful place in life."

I grabbed Nicolette by her river of dark hair and pulled her face level with mine. "Get out of here. Leave your things behind. Keep clear of my house."

"You're not my mistress now, you don't tell me what to do. I can act as I please."

"Can you? If I call the Watch?"

"Not so easy yet, my sweet Cecile."

Then I saw the knife flash in her hand.

"For God's sake, Nicolette—"

"I had a chance with him, one chance."

"Drop that knife, you're crazy."

"Maybe—little you care."

"Drop it, Nic. Don't be stupid."

She grabbed me. "Not stupid enough."

"What's that supposed to mean?"

"Not stupid enough to kill you."

"Then let me go." I tried to break her grip.

"Oh, I may." She spoke as if she had pepper on her tongue. "But first, I will make you ugly, so ugly, he won't want you anymore." Nicolette was laughing, a strange shrill sound in her throat. "No man will want you when I'm done with you, Cecile."

Her knife came at my cheek. I twisted away but she was fast. All at once, she pushed me face-down on the ground and straddled me. I felt her grabbing at my head as the knife flashed in the moonlight. Then I heard a strange sound behind me.

Nicolette was sawing off my hair; fistfuls of it fell to the ground beside my face. The knife was sharp and she was in a fever of destruction, hacking at my waist-long spill of curls. "There," she panted. "There. And there."

Her frenzy was so great, she cut her own fingers as she worked; her blood fell on my neck. More blood, more hair falling all around us in this ordinary lane, next to an ordinary rain barrel.

As Nicolette grew more frantic, she seemed winded and her strength appeared to wane. I drew on all of mine and heaved her off my spine. Then, grabbing her wrist, I bent back the hand gripping that honed blade.

At last, the knife fell with a simple thud onto the ground. Opposite each other, we crouched there in the dark, the knife between us. Nicolette summoned one more burst of rage.

With an animal's low cry, Nicolette sprang up and came at me with her nails, but I felt something surge within, fury I never knew was there. I slapped her hard across the face with the flat of my hand. She gasped, not expecting this from me.

Another stinging slap and she was down; I held her there with one knee. My fingers scrabbled about on the ground until I had the knife. She saw that and she saw my eyes and she did not try to rise.

"Go. Now." I threw the words at her.

"Damn you." Her voice rasped.

"Don't come home," I reminded her.

"As if I might beg your forgiveness?"

"Leave town now or face the *bâilli*."

I watched her for some moments. She did not move or speak as she tried to get her breath. Finally, shaken to the bone, I lurched off. Every third step I glanced back as Nicolette hunkered down on that patch of torn ground in the lane.

She did not make to follow me nor did she rise while she was still within my sight. The last time I glanced back, I saw her sitting in the moonlight with my hair scattered like weeds over her skirt.

The Night Watch would find her if she didn't get herself up and away. And she would, I knew. A scrappy survivor, she would find a pitying innkeeper who might believe she had been robbed. Soon enough, she would set her face toward the Paris road.

Turning the corner, I looked behind me once again. Nothing moved. There was only moonlight silvering the houses of Chartres and it curved around its hill. The town was still; from the earth there rose the sweet green smell of freshly scythed grass.

Still, I ran down one lane and turned into a different one and waited there until I knew that I was safe. The quiet was ordinary. A sleepy bird made a faint twitter. From an upstairs window, someone emptied a chamber pot. I realized I was shaking.

With one hand, I felt for my hair: she had hacked at it in an uneven circle. I had ringlets around my face but no lush curls rippled down my back. Those curls, I knew, were scattered like petals on that narrow back lane.

And what had Nicolette left me?

Tears filled my eyes. My hair was ravaged and I bled from one cheek and one arm. What was left of my tunic and skirt were torn and covered in mud. All that was true but true, too, was this. Later, I would not be found with my throat cut. I should be thanking God.

There was nothing to be done about my looks. Stupid of me, I thought, to fret about my hair when I still had my life. I staggered on, surprisingly unhurt, moving step by step toward home. The scratches on my arms began to sting. My numbness was wearing off. Sharper than any sting, deeper than any cut, I knew, were a friend's betrayal.

Once more I ran my fingers through my hair, hopeful that Gabriel would still find some bit of beauty left in me.

■

M on Dieu." He leapt to his feet when I crossed the threshold of our house. "Cecile, Cecile. What happened to you?"

"Nicolette." I was shaking now. "She tried to make me ugly for you. So you wouldn't want me."

"You? Never. Attacked, did she?"

Gabriel led me up the stairs into the solar which looked oddly untouched and ordinary.

"Now tell me, love." He sat me down.

I managed to rattle out what happened.

"Damn. Demon of a girl. Mad."

"She fought like a mad thing."

"Best she not come here."

"I don't think she will."

Prudently, he locked the door.

"Cecile, you're hurt. Don't say 'No.'"

"The blood's mostly hers, she cut herself while she was hacking at me. My face, my arm, the scratches aren't bad. They won't leave scars. I'm to rights somehow, I think." My voice shook now. "But my hair—"

He ruffled it. "You look like a cherub."

"You're trembling. And lying."

I picked up a hand mirror and winced at my reflection. It looked worse in the lamplight.

"Lying," I repeated. "Shamelessly."

"Trembling, yes. Lying, no." He held me close and rocked me and slowly we quieted.

"Blood all over you. That makes me tremble," he said. "Fear of losing what's so dear, that too. Nicolette, where is she now?"

"Out there somewhere. I told her to leave town. Now, tonight. I think she will, best let her be."

"Hard to do. Hate seeing you like this."

"A shorn sheep, no cherub."

"Beautiful." His lips brushed mine.

"I want...." I took a breath.

"What? Anything, Cecile."

"I can't say... I'm afraid you'll laugh."

"No laughing." He made a sober face. "You'd tell me 'No' if it's unseemly?"

"Yes. In advance. No conditions."

"I want." I felt sillier than before.

"What, my muddy cherub?"

"I want the man I love..."

"He's listening, Cecile."

"...to give me a bath."

For a moment he said nothing. I wondered if I'd spoken too boldly, too foolishly, or both.

"I'm being silly." I flushed.

"Not at all." I saw then how tense his face was, his jaw muscles working, and the pain in his steady eyes. The pain and the relief. Then his smile.

"A bath. I could manage that."

"Gabriel? You're certain?"

" One bath—for two?"

"That's even better."

Gabriel took off the cord around his neck. His mother's ring always hung there, day and night. Now he slid the thin band off its chain.

"Come, my Cecile." He led me to the table and there he turned to face me, holding my two hands in his. I didn't ask what he was doing. I knew. On the table were wild daisies in the old blue pitcher and three or four lit candles.

This, of course, would be our altar now; I read that in his face. We pledged ourselves once more. Then Gabriel slipped the ring on the second finger of my left hand.

From the pitcher, he pulled out two flowers, scattering their petals over us and to me the room looked taller, wider; soaring. It seemed oddly beautiful, with its benches and its buckets: such ordinary things, not ordinary after all.

Gabriel handed me a broom: the symbol of a married woman, mistress of the house. You see it still, tied to bridal carts. I held the broom as a queen would hold her rod of office.

Then I turned it flat across my upturned palms. Over the broom, I kissed Gabriel and so, in our own way, in our own time and place, we confirmed our vows, said our prayers, and again offered our thanks.

I added one petition: May Nicolette and all roving evil stay away from us throughout this night.

■

My nudity, since I was twelve, was hidden from everyone, except when I had fever as a child and a priest gave me the Last Rites too soon. Unready to die, I had sprung stark naked from my covers when I felt the Holy Oils on my forehead. This startled the young cleric who bolted, muttering to himself.

A woman, of course, guards her nudity, her modesty, until her marriage and even after that, most mothers once advised. Even my aunt included this ancient bit of caution:

Before venturing into the marriage bed, even after many years, I was warned to keep my night shift laced until all the lamps were out; all the shutters were closed.

Only when the chamber went dark could I slip—still in my shift—under the covers, which must reach as high as my chin, even in high summer. This was common guidance for young girls in my youth.

True, many men sleep naked—so I'd heard—but I was warned me to rest in bed with my arms folded across my breasts and my ankles crossed. How did conceptions manage to occur, I wondered, but never dared to ask.

I write this not in a spirit of self-disclosure but to show unwary readers just how bold I was. My request for a bath broke the rules of female modesty and maternal warning. The Church itself would condemn us if we were not wed, and so we felt we were. Vowed, wed, and witnessed—twice.

This was no childish play; nothing casual or common about it. And it was one of those times that bound us together, he and I, like the frame that holds the glass into a window.

For a moment, before he undressed me, Gabriel cupped my face in his hands, as he so loved to do, and scanned the scratches there. Gently, he wiped them clean of blood and, seeing how shallow they were, he sighed again with relief.

While the water heated over the kitchen fire, he peeled off my muddy outer tunic and slowly moved my long chemise. As it whispered to the floor, his fingers stroked their way around my waist as if to trace it.

Then he ran one finger over my outline, from the top of my head, along my neck and shoulders, down my side and legs until he reached my feet. He ran his finger up the other side of me until he reached my head, as if he wanted to draw me in the air—and remember the drawing.

On his knees, he drew off my shoes and rolled down my stockings, one leg, then the other; each gesture, careful, deliberate and cherished. He kissed my insteps and my ankles and my knees, scraped and rough, and then the soft flesh of my inner thighs.

A tingling passed through me, then a flash of heat. Between my thighs, above my thighs, his lips brushed me, and his hand reached up to remove my shift. At last, I stood naked before him.

He remained there on his knees before me, looking up and up and up, his eyes touching me here, then there, seeing through the mud and scrapes, seeing me as a whole.

His gray gaze lingered on my breasts. He stood up to kiss each one as if he were tasting grapes, and all the while I felt the flame that grows within. For some moments we stood there so, looking at each other. There were so many words, unspoken, passing between us. The room grew warm with them and with our gazing.

"Wanted you," he said at last. "Wanted you so long, my Cecile. So long, so much, I can't think how to tell you."

"And so I wanted you." I whispered; his touch had somehow taken away my voice. "I dare not say how long it's been my wish."

"Dare now. This is the night to dare with words. And other ways." He filled the great wash barrel with the water he had heated. "Tell me, my Cecile. Tell me how long, how much."

"From that first night at the top of the South Tower." Naked, I stepped into the barrel. "When you pulled me back."

"As I did." His wet hands slid over me.

"And a thousand times since."

"So it was with me, my love."

"You're watching me. As an artist?"

He laughed. "As a man. A lover."

Gabriel wet a cloth and wrung it out over my chest, so the water ran in rivulets between my breasts. This he did again, again; then he wrung the wet cloth so the water ran between my legs.

His fingers caressed me there and they were soft and they were firm as they moved deeper and I cried out; my body was hot now, even naked.

And so he bathed me, touching every inch of my skin; a gentle touch, as when a child is bathed— and yet not like a child at all. Soon his passion was as strong as his tenderness.

I loosed Gabriel's clothes. He dropped them to the floor and let me see his bared body in the fire light. After he stepped into the great barrel with me, I wrung the cloth out over him, so the water ran over his shoulders; lower then, between his thighs.

Wet and slick, we pressed together, standing in that circle of water, and he slipped himself between my legs while his mouth found mine. We were wrapped together there, our skin glistening.

I bent to him like a sapling in a summer breeze. He licked the water's trail between my breasts and took my fingers, one by one, into his mouth and then I kissed each of his.

Before we grew cold, he stepped out of the barrel to get his cloak. He wrapped me in it once more, as he had done when we were caught in that early morning's sudden rain.

From the barrel he led me out and up the stairs. His arm came under my legs and back, as he carried me to bed. Our lips clung as we pressed into the soft mattress and, lying in each other's arms, I felt his heat and he felt mine.

Gabriel's fingers were firm and his body was hard and we were lost in a dance that was ours, ours alone. Over and over, he whispered my name as he moved slowly, gently, to fill me.

Then his lips pressed mine and we were tasting each other in a new and deeper way. How we tingled and trembled with the power of each small movement; we, so joined, fit together as if we had been designed and crafted to be so.

As Gabriel kissed me again, he eased himself deeper inside me, taking care I felt no virginal pain. There was only the rhythm of the way he rocked me, whispering my name again and I whispered his.

We moved into a new dance then, where we arched and clung and swayed, until there was nothing, nothing but this, until he seemed to explode within me and my body answered his.

Later, we could not sleep for the nearness of each other and the hold of gaze on gaze, as strong and sensual as the dance itself. His mouth pressed mine again as he drew me nearer, and the taste of him was warm and salty-sweet; it seemed a taste that I had always known.

I kissed his eyes, their shifting grays, and the wisp of dark hair on his chest, and then below his chest. His hands were in my hair, tumbling it and smoothing it and loving it in all its tousled choppiness, and when I kissed between his legs, he cried out; a low long sound I will always hear.

Now Gabriel drew my face back up to his and, kissing it all over, even those few scratches, he moved in a fever of love, his hands cupping my breasts and stroking them in circles.

The circles grew smaller and tighter, until his fingers found each nipple, and then he caressed them with his tongue. I gasped again as he pressed his lips between my breasts and down my body as if he would drink it in like wine.

I swayed against him. His hand moved down and stroked between my legs, as he had done before, but now there was a difference, an urgency, a wildness. His touch was strong and sweet and searing and I was crying out as he filled me again

We were lost in each other, found in each other, and we were a long time in that dance, until we slept and woke to each other once more. The sky began to change, to shift, to lighten, and we sighed, watching the light grow.

We could not believe the night had passed and already we longed for afternoon, for the quiet time after work was done; for more time together in this bed, this placeless place where he took me and I took him and where we took each other.

"Come away with me," he whispered.

"Running off. I've dreamed of it."

"Dreams. Mine, too. Disappearing with you into Italy. Maybe Spain. Starting afresh."

"I'd go with you in a heartbeat, my love."

"Can't let you marry Morrisot—can't let him steal you from me. I hope he's given over that idea."

"Who is Morrisot?" I murmured the question into Gabriel's chest. On such a night I could make light of anything, however ominous.

Our laughter seemed to dart and dip like fireflies around the room, lighting here, lighting there, catching the new sun.

"If he took you I would be a monk for life."

"The Bishop must have disapproved the suit, there's been no talk of it," I said. "If any word is law, it's the Bishop's, and you've won him over."

"So I hope for both our sakes, Cecile."

"If he did not give consent, it cannot be, that marriage. He will want Morrisot's money for the windows, that won't change. 176 windows from you: that should be more than enough for them."

"If we ran off, I would leave behind each window, designed and laid out in detail. With you I can do such work." He paused. "I never thought to be loved so, Cecile."

"A lifetime commission?" I smiled.

"Just so, M'amselle, just so."

He ran his hand over my collarbone and again, between my breasts. "Now. I must find the blue. The one they want. I want. I promised that." He sighed. "If we left, I must leave it, too."

The sky itself was starting to turn blue.

But the wrong blue.

"If we left." I drew a breath. "I would break my promise to Our Lady. The first night I met you at the ruins, you heard it, I'm sure." I took a breath. "I promised I would give my dearest thing, my greatest gift if that would raise the cathedral up again, in more glory than ever before."

"Would Our Lady not see all you have already given, Cecile—time, love, effort, tears?"

"Our Lady would be merciful, I believe." I paused, thinking on an earthly level. "The Bishop and Morrisot would *not*."

"They're men, not God, *Cherie*."

"Men are often less merciful than God." I tried to make my words as gentle as I could. "If Morrisot still wants my hand and makes that a condition for the windows, he would hunt us if we fled."

"Hunt us?" He shook his head.

"Us." I felt something twist inside me. "Those brothers would destroy your reputation. You'd never work again. How I pray the suit is dropped."

We heard my stepfather stirring in his bed-chamber above but his snoring went on.

"It would be hard, leaving these windows," Gabriel said after a moment. "Letting someone else piece them and watch them swung into their frames. But it would be far harder to leave you, my Cecile. Does any window equal what we have?"

We watched the last of the night drain from the sky. Never had I regretted the sight of dawn before. Everything, even the floor-boards, looked different to me now.

As the morning light touched us, I knew we were changed. The very colors of our bodies and our souls were altered by this wind-like sweep of feeling: no wisp of air, no whim.

"To part from you." I looked into his eyes; I had never gazed at him so deeply, so directly nor had he gazed ever that way at me. Such looks could be indiscreet, inviting trouble. And we had started out together in the dark; there raw feelings could be veiled and protected.

From the beginning, we had to remain so careful around each other, we felt easier and a bit safer with out stolen, sideways glances. But after tonight nothing was the same, nor could it be again.

"To part from you...." My eyes filled.

"Cecile." He sounded abrupt.

"What's happened? Say it."

"Look at me." The artist's command.

"What's wrong?" I was almost frightened.

"There it is. Right before me. All this time." He was on his feet, lifting my hand-mirror. "See?"

Puzzled, I took the mirror and glanced into it. I noted my sleepy face, my tearful gaze, my choppy hair. "I don't know...tell me."

"Look now." His smile was once again an open door. "Why is it we never notice?"

"What?" I felt thick in the head.

"Notice what's right in front of us."

He cupped my face with his hands.

"I think you've noticed me tonight."

"Yes. And no. All this time I saw *you*, my Cecile. Saw with a lover's sight. You, as a whole. Never stopped to analyze you, piece by piece. Until now when it stared me in the face."

I still didn't take his meaning.

"How I've searched. Everywhere but here. Right here. Look again, my love."

I stared into the hand mirror. There was my scratched face. My horrible hacked hair.

"I don't know what—"

And then at last I saw:

Blue! Gabriel's new blue.

It was the color of my eyes.

My eyes, on him. ∎

W ith that blue we won—and lost.

Weeks passed quickly after Gabriel's discovery. Now his work would have its final judgment by the prelates, the priests, the powerful locals of this town.

At my post in the storeroom of the Bishop's Palace, I looked out the window. From there I watched a lengthy processional of white-garbed clerics winding like a sash across the green of early August grass.

Banners flew.

Heads bowed.

Patrons paced.

Behind this procession trudged a stream of townspeople, hundreds of them, like pilgrims once again, as we were the night we pulled those carts from the old stone quarry.

Somehow this contest had again lit a keen interest in the cathedral's rise. The Master

Sculptor's commission had been made some time before. The Master of Works, we knew, was now in place. This day would see the last of the great commissions—so it was hoped. And this day was Gabriel's last chance to become a Master at Chartres. Or not.

Wagers rode on today's outcome. No one could overlook the fevered curiosity throughout the town. The Master Glazier would be only one of our cathedral's artists—but his part, perhaps, looked the most magical, even miraculous.

Soaring vaults and arches and great sculpture were highly prized and stirred the soul. These, of course, were valued and venerated: the cathedral's bones and flesh: true enough.

Even so, light-struck glass seemed other-worldly: windows open on another place, a better place, beyond the earth. Stained glass figures, with their gem-like colors, appeared alive, as if they could look out and breathe and speak.

Their pictures told the story of God's people, so they spoke to us. Those many panels showed us who we were, and who we are, and who we might become. Such figures were fragile, like men and women, but they would outlast us all. They mirrored a mystery. But who would make them?

Everyone wanted to know.

Everyone had a favorite.

Everyone had a guess.

"The young one," as people now referred to Gabriel. "That young glass-maker" might well stay here and give the cathedral "its eyes," as some called the windows. It would be a marvel if he could, his backers said. Many would watch those windows emerge

Still more marvelous, they added, this man was not only gifted, he was of an age to see most of his windows through to their completion—within the lifetimes of many who worshiped here.

Those who disapproved of color or of Gabriel or both had other notions. "Too young, too inexperienced .bright, too new." We had heard it all before. One way or another, this would be a day to mark and speak about to coming generations.

The "New Blue" itself would be shown for the first time today. Along with samples of other stained glass windows, this original shade would be on display. The viewing would take place in the Great Hall of the Bishop's Palace—now.

I hoped our guests knew they would see only sample sections of great windows, not the finished work. That would be impossible here in the Bishop's Great Hall: a full window could be ten or twenty feet tall. Gabriel had designed what would fit this space and his workmen took great pains to bring these samples here.

How hard Gabriel had worked for this moment. All the while I was baking bread in my ovens, he was making glass in his. For many weeks, he had spent much of each day with his workmen at the glass-makers' forest "studio."

These men were skilled artisans, Gabriel knew well. They could start now to turn his designs into pieced stained glass, strong enough to last for centuries. Hard to believe such things could come from a mix of ash and sand, heat and wit, metal and minerals—and talent. As a baker, oddly enough, I understood.

The crucibles had waited when Gabriel had begun to measure out the cobalt and his "secret salts" for his formula. As the molten glass was heated, he watched it closely; these hues, he said, were volatile. Everything could change with higher heat and lengthened time. I saw this happen myself. Who would think yellow could turn into lavender?

It was in the forest that Gabriel had found the precise amounts of the ingredients he wanted, heated at a certain temperature, for an allotted time. There, among the beech trees, he created that different blue he so desired: conjured from his "secrets" and from cobalt, heat and soda lime glass.

He was far from pleased with the shade of his first "gathers," once they were blown into cylinders, reheated and spread into sheets. He had studied the glass, then tried different formulas with different heat levels and timing.

This color must be exact, even if he had to change the formula a hundred times. I could feel Gabriel's frustration on the days he took me out into the forest. There he would gaze directly into my eyes for some time. Then he was back about his work.

He still came to our house to sleep. Now it seemed safe to be together there; my stepfather always drank himself to bed and Nicolette, of course, was gone. Morrisot no longer haunted us; there seemed no reason for us to fear him now.

After days of such exacting work, Gabriel needed a nightly escape; this he found in my arms and in my bed. Once released, our passion for each other never weakened; rather it intensified and our lovemaking I think, was a release for both of us.

One afternoon, when at last the desired blue appeared, a messenger from the forest came running to me at the bakery. I followed the lad directly to the glass-makers' workplace. There Gabriel caught me in his arms and swung me in a circle. His workmen smiled at their Master. He did not care who saw us then. And he did not need to speak.

There, too, in the outdoor workplace, Gabriel and his men made and fired other sheets of colored glass—one a glowing red made, in part, from blood and wineskins, and a white from tin filings, antimony, and arsenic. Here again were precise measures of molten glass, metals, salts, heat, design—and talent.

At last the glass was annealed, cut, painted, and set into the lead cames that held a sample's pieces together. I had seen the new glass and marveled—but now that all was finished, Gabriel, still worried, paced within our house. The waiting, I believe, was even harder than the work.

Finally, I took him to the Bishop's palace through the servants' door and up the backstairs to the storeroom over part of the Great Hall where the judges' decision would be made—not soon enough, of course, for us.

Earlier, as I had confessed, the storeroom's floor had been my hidden post for spying on the hall below, whether it was set for a banquet or a formal dinner, or a reception for certain visitors: scholars, perhaps, or clergy, or dignitaries.

I watched as Gabriel stooped through the low doorway of my hiding place and I had to smile at the sight of him there—where I had seen him first. He looked about him at the barrels lining one top wall and noted the floor's cracks and knotholes.

Now, at this anxious moment, Gabriel would spy with me, if I could keep him from pacing back and forth; this he must not do or his repeated steps could be heard below. As would our voices. We did not dare to speak.

In pained suspense, Gabriel must wait up there until the hall was filled and then he would go down to stand beside his work. I would stay here alone and watch him through the cracks and knotholes of the storeroom's floor.

This time, of course, there was no banquet—rather, a trial of sorts. I remembered how nervous I had been the night of the Bishop's feast where I saw Gabriel. That feeling seemed a ripple compared to the waves I felt today. I felt each wave within me, as if they might break through my skin.

Gabriel must have felt this all the more. His hand closed over my fidgety fingers. Once again I asked myself if it was good to love someone this much. And once again, the answer came back. What does it matter, in the end? It simply is.

We had heard the guests entering, milling about, then settling. We chose not to watch just yet. Before he went downstairs, Gabriel ran his fingers through my hair. He held me to him as a clasp holds a cloak together and so we swayed there, amid bins and barrels until we heard the hall grow quiet. We looked at each other. It was time, we knew.

I kissed his fingers and sent him down and after he had gone, I felt I might fly apart with frustration. I could not pace—or be discovered. Nor could I make myself peer through the floor's knotholes and cracks. I'd be unable to stay calm if I watched the scene unfolding below.

And so I crouched there, listening, hoping to hear some word, some sign of judgment. There was a wind-like sigh and some rustling. The Bishop, with a fanfare, was announced.

The Great Hall held many guests: The Bishop's assistants, the members of the Cathedral Chapter the Cathedral School and rest of the clergy. All I heard now was the whispering of vestments. A cough. A mouse. And my own heartbeat.

I counted to sixty.

Then sixty again.

I listened for applause.

All I heard was silence.

Had I gone stone deaf?

I put my ears to the floor.

Still nothing. Not a word.

More dead cold silence.

Angry, I kept listening.

I dared not to look quite yet; not until I had myself in hand. Crouching high above the Great Hall, I prayed in silence—and imagined. The many clerics and certain patrons were still studying the new colored glass. What was taking so long?

Earlier, I had dared to offer one suggestion: I thought the five samples should be hung in front of the existing windows, all of them clear, so the colored glass could glow as sunlight poured into the hall. Gabriel had surveyed the space and had the new samples rehung before the clear panes.

There was nothing else I could do then but try to be steady and wait. And there I stood above the judges and where I listened so intently I thought I heard dust settling. The silence grew longer still. I had the sickening sensation I'd known as a child, almost falling from a tree I'd climbed.

Minutes passed, several minutes; perhaps a quarter-hour. Tears stung my eyes. Gabriel had labored with such passion, such intensity, such skill, he deserved more than this block of icy silence.

At last I took hold of myself and I knelt on the floor. I held back another moment and then put my eye to a wide crack. Peering down, I caught my breath. I looked again and then I lay flat on the wooden boards so I could get a wider view of the Great Hall below.

Through the floor's cracks and then through a knothole, I saw a space transformed by light, as if the hall had come unmoored from earth and floated in the highest reaches of the skies. This was now another country, glimpsed only in dreams.

The whole place was bathed in blue—the blue Gabriel had sought so long. In that Great Hall, that grand space, his creations remained strong and true, lit and glowing as the sun filtered through.

And there was something more. On separate panels were the figures of two women made of pieced stained glass: one was Lady Libra with her scales and one, I knew, was Eve, holding an apple in her hand. The glass-painting on these two figures was exquisite and detailed. I recognized their faces as my own. No one else appeared to notice.

Light spilled through other colors, too, turning one wall into the brilliant red of a summer sunrise. Another, the shimmer of a lush meadow's greens. The gold of cats' eyes. The purple of dusk. But that blue, otherworldly, and yet human—its presence transformed everything it touched.

In a mysterious way, this color appeared to move over the hall and the hall seemed to breathe, to inhale and exhale blue, as the sunlight shifted outside. On the wall, the Great Cross itself was bathed in this serene and splendid glow.

If God's love could be glimpsed in glass, I thought, surely this had happened here. The blue was more than a color. It was, indeed—a gaze.

Held within that gaze the Great Hall had become sacred space: the nave of an incomparable and yet unseen cathedral. That early hush, so long, so broad, was something I now understood.

It was worship's silent music. ∎

W e had won indeed.
I saw Gabriel standing at the far end of the hall and now at last there came words of praise and admiration; as I listened to them, I felt them in every sinew, every bone.

Everyone was of the same mind: Praise rose as the colors shifted with the interplay of sun and clouds. The town seemed far away, though it lay just beyond this sky-struck, God-struck place.

For a moment, a new cloud must have passed before the sun, bringing a bit of twilight into the hall. This shade had its own otherworldly beauty, mystical and moving; it caused another hush.

Then the cloud swept away. The sun blazed like blue fire through the glass and a gasp rose from the assembled company. It was some time before words come to anyone again.

After the clergy and patrons had filed out into the daylight, I waited in the storeroom, hoping

Gabriel would come back up. Soon, we knew, he would be called outside and lauded before the whole town—next week there would be a banquet, toasts, and speeches. But first, we would have some private time, whichever way the verdict went.

Now I heard Gabriel's familiar steps on the storeroom stairs and then he was there. Someone had given him a bouquet of wild flowers and these he gave to me. I was amazed that he had come at all—in fact, when he stepped into the storeroom, I was just rising, somewhat unsteadily, from the wooden floor.

Gabriel lifted me to my feet as if he were, indeed, breaking a fall once more. When the last invited guests had gone, he drew me to him with such force it seemed that we would meld together, fused like glass in heat beyond our own.

And so we stood when Jean Morrisot appeared in the storeroom. Distracted, we had not heard his step, else he was stealthy. As he came in we turned our heads as one. Outside the people were calling Gabriel's name, chanting, cheering.

"In a few moments, you must go down to them," Morrisot told him. "However." That pause, as ever, was chilling. "Before you do, there are weighty matters to settle. And loose threads to snip."

Snip? I did not like that word.

Nor did I like Morrisot's tone.

"I have caught you out at last," he said.

"Blame me," Gabriel said. "Not Cecile."

"No blame, Sir." Morrisot cut him off. "I salute you both. Everything has happened as I hoped."

We stared at him but did not move apart.

"The cathedral's glory is assured." In Morrisot's pale face, his eyes appeared triumphant and for once, only that once, did they glimmer. "We shall have stained glass windows to surpass all others. Their holiness and beauty: indisputable."

"My pledge to you." Gabriel's voice was firm.

"Indeed. But I must speak plainly, sir." Morrisot turned to face him. "Three months ago I was unsure of you. But now you understand; you feel what you create." The older man steadied his voice. "You question me?"

"One thing. Most important." Gabriel spoke now. "The new Master of Works. He will build with walls of glass in mind?"

"We have decided on a man of high repute who will build as Bonnet wished. I know this choice is right. Perhaps even for the best."

I braced for Morrisot's next words.

"The people shall glimpse God's loving gaze in glass," he went on then. "A gaze known, in part, through human love. Now this love is alive within the glass, as I wished it to be. And so...."

Another pause, longer than the first.

"The Bishop shall have his windows—and my promised funds." Morrisot looked directly at Gabriel. "You, sir, shall have your commission for as long as you live. The Bishop has persuaded Henri Dufort to donate all his extra space as a workshop for your glaziers. There many of your new windows will be made." He took a breathe. "As patron of a such great windows, I shall be well remembered."

Morrisot shifted his tall frame in the cramped space and there, in the dimness of the storeroom, I saw into his mind. He had thought to foster Gabriel's love for me and so create surpassing art: the loving gaze of God reflected in our own.

Underneath my fear lay fury. Morrisot could not take credit for our love. It was kindled by us, not by this man. His forbearance had been needed; I gave him that. He had guarded and protected what already flowed between us and was then set forever.

I still believed Jean Morrisot thought of himself as the hidden author of the great windows to come. And I knew he would want his payment now. In his mind, this was his just and deserved reward. I was ready when he spoke again.

"And you, Cecile? What shall you have?"

"My desired husband," I was bold to say.

"I shall have my desired wife," Morrisot countered. "Cecile, the Bishop was so impressed with your defense of M'sieur le Glazier, His Excellency has altered his views. He now consents to the marriage."

For one more second, I gripped my last mad hope. And then I felt it slip like water through my fingers. I bit my lip. I would not let this hollow man draw tears from me. Not here, not ever.

"*Our* marriage." Gabriel was firm.

"No, sir. *Our* marriage." Morrisot spoke with a king's authority. "I will wed Cecile Dufort in Paris."

"No—never." Gabriel's voice stung.

"You, M'sieur, have nothing to do with it."

"I have everything to do with it, I love her."

"Of course." Morrisot voice hardened. "Hence the loving gaze within your new and dazzling blue. Indeed, within all of your stained glass. That love is in your eyes—and in M'amselle Cecile's."

"I waited until this last test was past." Gabriel's voice was taut. "Today I will present a marriage contract to be signed."

"You are too late, M'sieur." Morrisot gave his wintry smile. "Cecile's father and the Bishop gave their consent to *me*. The contract was signed and witnessed early this morning."

"Surely, Sir." I was pleading now. "Surely, the windows are enough for you."

"Ah, you forget your place, Cecile. You forget your debt to me." Morrisot was curt. "It was I who kept you safe, the two of you, these last months. In a moment I could have destroyed you both."

There was a long silence; then Morrisot's regal voice went on. "Think what I could tell my brother, the Bishop. I, his brother, not a housemaid. You would be finished, M'sieur Gabriel. Utterly finished. As you would be, M'amselle Cecile."

A deep pit of silence.

"Blackmail." Gabriel said, finally.

"If you like." Morrisot was unruffled. He tented his fingers together and surveyed us for some moments. "Do not try to run away together—I know your minds better than you may imagine."

"Let me speak—" Gabriel began.

"*You* listen to *me*." Morrisot cut him off.

We had no choice; had we, ever?

And so Morrisot went on.

"Gabriel." Another hard look from the older man. "Would you really forfeit this prize commission? Would you disgrace your name? Sacrifice your reputation and your chance to work anywhere again? I have a long reach, as does my brother. Would you choose us as enemies?"

Morrisot left a strained silence. Then, as I expected, he made a slow turn to look at me.

"And you, Cecile" His eyes were bright in his gaunt face. "Would you shame your Gabriel and block the use of his great gifts? Would you shame your family? Cheat thousands of pilgrims yet to come?"

Morrisot's looked at us both.

"Would you dishonor Our Lady?"

A silence entered the room like an intruder, a thief, a pickpocket at a fair. It stood with us, it muted us, and in its presence, we heard Morrisot's words repeat themselves as if he spoke again.

There was nothing to be done.

All would have to be as this man had arranged so carefully—our patron, our protector, oddly enough. Anyone else would have had me flogged and turned out and Gabriel banished before now. We all knew this. But I made one desperate appeal.

"You wanted a beautiful wife." I took off my shorn head's covering. "I am no beauty now."

"Hair is naturally replaced."

"Love is not," I burst out.

"I do not imagine, M'amselle, that you will love me. I do not ask that of you. I demand your presence, your company. And an end to my loneliness."

"Can you expect my love?" I asked.

"You will always love your Gabriel, that I know, and he, you." Morrisot pointed a thin finger at me. "But you *will* give me and your Bishop due respect. It is an even-handed bargain. You will protect Chartres—and each other."

He almost smiled.

Almost.

I swallowed the tears in my throat.

"Ready yourself, Cecile." Morrisot's voice hovered near the borders of kindness. "I take you now to Paris. There we wed. Say your goodbyes and then, Gabriel, you will come down and greet the crowds."

Morrisot stooped through the storeroom door, then turned. "I will be waiting outside for you. The *bâilli* and his men will wait as well."

He was gone.

■

To make a clean break in a piece of glass, it first must be scored, then gently tapped. That glass will comes apart quite easily. It is not so easy with two human beings who have melded into one. It is not easy at all.

Somehow I had always sensed this outcome awaited us. I knew it when I spoke out before the Bishop. But Gabriel and I would not have given up what we had, whatever pain it cost us. And pain there was. I cannot sweeten those few words.

That day, that final day, we stood together in that storeroom by its only window. There we held each other as if we stood in a strong wind, a gale that uproots trees and unroofs barns and tosses people into strange and distant fields.

We could not part; we could not stay. We could not let go and hold on at once. But even in the coming years, filled with daily letters, we would be one. Fused glass is remarkably strong.

"You will be with me," Gabriel said finally.

"And you with me—it cannot change."

"I stand bereaved. But not alone."

"Never that." I tried for a weak smile.

"Not for us." His forehead touched mine.

"Not for us." I said that to hear it again.

"He won't let us meet. That he can prevent."

"He cannot. I will see you everywhere."

"And I you, Cecile, my love."

We held each other and I let him go.

As I heard his steps move slowly down the stairs, I shut my eyes. Then, wiping my face, I moved to the storeroom window for one more look at Gabriel, my "dark friend," and yes, to me, my husband.

Below, I saw him step out into the sun and the thrilled crowd. I watched the breeze stir his hair; and the sleeves of his blue tunic. The people cheered.

But Gabriel's eyes were not with them. Turning, looking up, he scanned the palace wall behind him. Quickly, he found what he sought: the window where he knew I would be standing.

That day I wore red, for luck. Gabriel's eyes fixed on the color, then on my face. He was just below me as I raised my hand to him and his hand lifted high as if to catch hold of mine once more.

I hold that picture of him in my mind. In his mind, I knew, he would always see me, bright with color, framed and held for him forever in a window.

■

CHARTRES, FRANCE
1196

After two long years, I have come back to Chartres. The cathedral is well begun and I delight in its progress; but this is not my only reason for returning. As I said, I wanted to see what was here for me once and what might yet be here for me.

My arrival in the town has been expected. News of death flies faster than a falcon. Everyone in Chartres knows I am now a widow and one of ample means, they might add. They *will* add, of course.

Jean Morrisot was taken ill at our wedding feast in Paris. Stricken suddenly, he never quite recovered —and never quite believed he was undone. He remained frail, tired easily and often lay abed. His heart was failing; the doctors could do nothing for him. His family's grand home was our residence. At times, I must admit, it felt like a prison to me.

As long as he could, Jean Morrisot kept his grip on life. A month ago, he died in that house where he was born. I had come to pity him; he had come to pity himself. His last year was a bitter time; as he weakened further, he raged at his fate.

Now he is at peace and I have settled his affairs. After all was finished properly, I hesitated for a few days, deciding what might lie ahead for me. Then I packed two chests and sent them on ahead to this, my town. I have only just arrived here.

Gabriel had stayed in Chartres with his faithful glass-makers. Together they labored on, preparing panels for the new cathedral's windows. The work was going well, Gabriel told me in his daily letters. In mine, I offered encouragement and, of course, my congratulations.

We wrote of many things, however small: morning mist, evening meals, midnight stars. A solitary walk, a solitary glass of wine. Good health, thank God, for both of us. A bit of gossip, here and there. Everything—except the future.

A sadness whispered through Gabriel's words to me. I feared he had once again withdrawn into himself as he had done before I met him. Perhaps he kept a shell of solitude about him, even as he worked with his glass-makers; even as he rented his room in the baker's house.

Gabriel proposed no plans for us to meet. I countered his silence on this subject with my own. We were always shy of risking refusals from each other; this I well remembered. Perhaps he awaited my invitation. Perhaps I was awaiting his. Perhaps he didn't want to say his life had moved on.

I never dared to ask him such things. I hardly dared to think them. And so, afraid of disappointment, I hesitated those few days before returning to Chartres. As soon as I arrived, I went directly to the new cathedral's building site.

There I stood, looking about with that intensity I mentioned earlier. Even so, I saw no sign of Gabriel. My veil had slipped from my hair, now bright in the sun. I dropped the veil and straightened my blue tunic—and still I hesitated to ask anyone for Master Glazier.

I turned and walked the few steps to the old cathedral's South Tower. Now, instead of ruins, it overlooked the building site. As I went inside, a gust of wind slammed the tower's door behind me: a jolt, that *thunk,* followed by its long and rising echo.

Ahead of me, the spiral staircase wound upwards. I paused. Moments passed. My eyes grew used to the dimness of the place, sliced with sunlight from its narrow windows. My climb had to begin.

I took a breath. A step. And stopped. Above, I heard descending footfalls: familiar, recognizable. Each one sounded closer than the last. I listened to them quicken—nearer, clearer; nearer still.

And then I saw the white flash of his smile. Gabriel had rounded the spiral's nearest turn; he ran down the remaining stairs, his hand reaching for me as I moved toward him.

■

AUTHOR'S NOTE

"None can be found in the whole world that can equal [Chartres'] structure, its style and decor. None is shining so bright than this nowadays rising anew." William The Breton, Court Chartres, 1222.

About fifty miles southwest of Paris, rising from the cornfields of La Beauce, is Chartres, France. It is an ancient town, dating back to Roman times. The Cathedral Basilica Our Lady of Chartres has been an important pilgrimage destination for centuries. Enshrined there is a treasured relic, the *Sancta Camisa*, believed to be the childbirth tunic of the Virgin Mary.

It is estimated that five cathedrals rose consecutively at Chartres. On a hot and windy Friday night, the tenth of June, 1194, a raging fire damaged part of the town and destroyed much of its

Chartres Cathedral: view from southeast.

existing cathedral. The North and South Towers survived intact as did the West Wall with its sculpture and stained glass, as did the crypt, and the sturdy foundational structure.

Some sources attribute the fire's cause to a lightning strike on the North Tower but that report may be confused with such a strike in 1506 which destroyed this tower. There is no agreement on the cause of the fire in 1194.

Three days after this devastating event, Chartres' prized relic was found to be intact. From the cathedral's ruins, priests emerged with the *Sancta Camisa*. This discovery was seen as a sign and an inspiration for the town to raise another cathedral, even more splendid than its precedents; like them it would honor the Virgin Mary.

The burgeoning Gothic style of architecture would be used. The coming cathedral would reach higher and wider than previous structures. It would also contain great spaces for "walls of stained glass windows." These would become world-renowned for their brilliant gem-like colors.

Supporting the heavy lead roof, a brilliant system of columns, piers, and flying buttresses would open up the sanctuary to more light., seen by two deceased bishops (Suger and Fulbert) as a manifestation of the Divine Essence.

Drawn from France and the European continent, over 4,000 donors contributed to this celebrated project. These donors ranged from royalty to merchants to craftsmen. Forty-two tradesmen's confraternities donated stained glass windows, "signed" by tradesman's depictions.

We know nothing of the talented Masters who created the "new" Chartres Cathedral after the 1194 fire. Their work is not signed; their names and their personal histories have been lost, according to reliable sources. The cathedral is their signature.

Also unknown to us are the hundreds of laborers and gifted artisans who worked on the cathedral and contributed so much to its art and architecture. Their number varies with the sources.

It is important to note: The distinction between a glass-maker, a glass-painter, and a glazier, was *not* distinct in the early Middle Ages. I have used the term "Glazier" here as a generic designation.

About the "Chartres Blue:" the visionary Abbot Suger (1081-1151) created a special blue for stained glass. This may be referred to as the "Chartres Blue." However, the Abbot was deceased for almost a half-century when the 1194 cathedral was raised at Chartres. Its windows were newly created then; new color interpretations were likely. A highly reliable source detects a difference between the pre-1194 Blue and the post-1194 Blue.

The Master of Works (also known as the Master of Masons or Master of the Compasses, depending on the source) was the chief architect and overseer of the building process. This Master had a complex knowledge of geometry, engineering, and calculations made with plumb lines and compasses.

Another talented "Adept" (a medieval term) was commissioned as the Master of remarkable sculpture, rendered by many artists: over 4,000 statues, extensive *bas relief* and other carvings.

Yet another man was commissioned as the Master who designed and guided the creation of 176 stained glass windows, some over twenty feet high and six feet wide. It is important to note that the distinctions among glass-makers, glaziers, and glass-painters were *not* clearly or rigidly defined in the twelfth century. Glazier is a generic term used here to encompass the three categories.

The Master Glazier's designs were rendered, for the most part, by one or more traveling "studios" of assistant glass-makers who worked on-site. Teams of artisans set the windows into place. Chartres cathedral's complex windows (some fifty feet tall) were designed and rendered on a grand scale, as previously noted.

After the 1194 fire, the plans and execution of Chartres' new cathedral was of major importance to a variety of people. This extraordinary effort was of great interest to Pope Celestine III who dispatched a Papal Legate to Chartres in 1194, as the new cathedral was designed. The work itself proceeded with swift intensity.

Chartres' townsfolk, too, were zealous about raising the new sanctuary. Over 1,000 townsfolk carted building stones from the Bérchères quarry. In addition to oxen, donkeys, and horses, the people of Chartres were yoked to carts they pulled themselves. This unique event was called "The Cult of the Carts."

However, in France, there was debate over the use of color (and how much) in twelfth century sacred stained glass. One important reason for was the extra expense of more color and vivid color. In addition, the Gothic cathedral style was still coming into its own in 1194. Most previous cathedrals were Romanesque. This style had smaller windows and darker interiors. In addition, previous cathedrals had featured *Grisaille* windows (gray or colorless glass). Some criticism of vivid color in sacred glass was attributed, in part, to certain monastic orders.

The relative newness of the color blue in Northern Europe's sacred art is documented. Blue fell out of usage until the late tenth century. Gradually this color became associated with the Virgin Mary. Earlier, her garb was usually depicted as black to denote mourning.

Medieval stained glass was made by complex methods. These were described by Theophilus, a twelfth century Benedictine monk and artist. This novel attempts to capture some of his salient details without overwhelming the novel with too much technicality.

Grateful acknowledgment is also made for the invaluable material in *Glass-Painters* by Sarah Brown and David O'Connor.

Medieval architects and artists did "inscribe" or draw designs on chalked or plastered boards on high tables, first with lead, then with black or red paint. The designers used compasses and rulers for measurements. The paper "cartoon" for the overall design was not in use as early as 1194. Glassmakers did keep copybooks of previous designs.

For readers who have never been to Chartres, it may be difficult to conceptualize its windows. They rose to great heights (ten to twenty-seven feet tall in some cases) and depict numerous scenes from Scripture and from the lives of several saints.

These windows were (and are) not only beautiful, they were (and are) educational. Most medieval people were illiterate and learned the entire Bible from "reading" its scenes in the stained glass.

The first sacred stained glass depictions of the tradesmens' confraternities first appeared in the windows of Chartres Cathedral and Bourges Cathedral. The building of these two cathedrals were roughly contemporaneous. Some sources claim Chartres' trade windows were the earliest; this point may be debated.

There are several theories about the "tradesmen's windows," where ordinary craftsmen are depicted at their work. Medievalist Jane Welch Williams makes a case for the exclusive use of "stock images" (in seven poses) in Chartres Cathedral's trade windows.

An expert iconographer disagrees and notes more than seven poses. Other sources have theorized that some figures in the stained glass were designed from life. We don't know what kind of artistic discussions preceded such designs.

Chartres Cathedral is remarkable in numerous ways. One is the swiftness of its completion. Sources assert that many windows were in place by 1204-1210, perhaps even earlier. Most of the cathedral was finished about thirty years after the 1194 fire: approximately 1225, according to several sources.

After surviving the fire, the extant twelfth century West Wall, the Royal Portal, with its sculpture, glass and towers, was incorporated into the new sanctuary. One source suggests that its stained glass windows were damaged, then restored, then repainted.

However, John James, architect and seasoned Chartres expert suggests a different scenario. He believes the West Wall was part of a narthex, or entry, and its glass was protected by a partition, thus shielding the glass. Therefore, the glass was not damaged and did not have to be extracted, releaded, and restored, as the first source suggested.

According to Malcolm Miller, another long-time expert, there are no solid explanations for the survival of those earliest windows in the West Wall.

Advance designs preceded and kept pace with the construction. This speed gave Chartres Cathedral an unusually unified style. Most medieval cathedrals took a century or more to complete and decorate.

As noted previously the Cathedral of Our Lady of Chartres (according to many congruent sources) was essentially finished about 1223-1225, but the North Rose window, donated by Queen

Blanche of Castile and installed about 1235. The cathedral was consecrated in 1260 but may have been blessed before that date.

Chartres is remarkable in yet another way: it is one of the few medieval cathedrals to retain almost all of its original stained glass. Many other sanctuaries lost windows to wars, revolution and, to some degree, reformation. The splendor of Chartres Cathedral attracts 1.5 million visitors a year.

~~~

A few notes on medieval life and terms:

»Women did work as professional bakers, although they were excluded from membership in the craftsmen's "Confraternities."

»They also worked as glass-painters, e.g., "Agnes le glasenwryght." Many were glass-painters' widows.

»*bâilli* is the word for a French Medieval law enforcement officer comparable to a Reeve in Medieval England and a Sheriff (derived from Shire Reeve) in America.

»Banquets were often elaborate, including some of their fare and settings, as shown here.

»Strewn rushes may have covered bare floors but medieval expert, Susan Woodbury, makes an excellent case for woven rush mats instead.

»Trenchers were often made of thick bread. Medieval people usually ate unleavened bread. In France, yeast was only used for pastry.

»Metal forks and spoons were not available to France in 1194. Wooden spoons were. Knives were the common dining utensils.

»Beds' characteristics varied with social class. Some were based on a network of ropes; others on wooden slats. Feather mattresses were for the rich, though prosperous burghers could acquire them or inherit them.

»Glass windows were usually for the wealthy, the nobility, and high-ranking clergy. However, a wealthy burgher's house could have two or three with shutters to close or open.

»Many middle-class households had large wooden tubs for bathing or laundry.

»The "solar," a bed/sitting room, varied in size and topped the "Grand Hall" just below. In a small houses this hall might be less than "grand"—an entry space of varying sizes.

»Urine was used as a paint ingredient as well as a stain-solvent in the laundering process; potato skins were used to starch linen.

»Pottage was a common dish in medieval France: it was a thick vegetable soup or stew.

»The ballad's fragment sung by Cecile's aunt was of this novel's period. The song was written by a well-known poet, Marie de France.

»"Old French" was spoken in medieval France. I have tried to be sensitive to the blend of varied cadences from Old French, modern French, and American-accented English vernacular.

»Church Latin has predominated here over classical Latin where appropriate.

»The medieval administration of the Last Rites of the Roman Catholic Church (now renamed) differs in some respect from later rubrics.

» Rules of sexual conduct were ostensibly strict but, as always, subject to human interpretation, even in regard to some clerical cases.

»"Annealing," in glass-making, is a process of heating followed by slow cooling to strengthen the final product.

»The technical word "came" refers to a grooved metal framing structure to hold pieced glass in place.

»The famous labyrinth of Chartres was created around 1230, *after* the time-frame of this novel.

»Rush lamps, a kind of oil lamp, were frequently used in medieval homes. Except for the rich, beeswax candles were too expensive for everyday use in middle-class households. "Lanthorns" would hold less expensive candles made of animal tallow.

»A Cathedral Chapter is an ecclesiastical "college" or group which assists and advises the bishop. Its members included the Cathedral's canons or clergy.

»The term "Night Watch" sounds modern but such citizen's groups existed in French towns in the twelfth and thirteenth centuries.

~~~

»A note on vocabulary:
Peintre-Berrier: Glass-painter

Verrier: Glass-maker
Patisserie: Pastry.
Pâtissière: Female pastry chef.
Non pareil: Incomparable.
Vite: Quick.
Mon Dieu: "My God."
Sacre Bleu: A mild form of swearing.

~~~

It is important to note that this novel is *not* a history book. However, the novel was extensively researched *in* history books, in and around the Cathedral of Chartres and in interviews with experts.

I have had the privilege of walking, climbing, and standing where many of the novel's scenes unfold (including the South Tower). During my third and longest stay in Chartres (a month), I was immersed in the cathedral's ambience every day.

Visitors' reactions to its magic and its shifting lights and moods are unforgettable. I also learned a great deal from observing one of many pilgrimages and its ceremonial culmination at Chartres Cathedral.

Most valuable of all is what I learned from Malcolm Miller, the extraordinary author, scholar, lecturer, and expert on Chartres Cathedral. He has lived and worked in Chartres for some fifty years. I will always owe him a great debt of gratitude.

Mr. Miller taught me how to read the stories in the amazing stained glass windows. He offered me special guidance and insights regarding every facet of the sanctuary and its creation. I thankfully acknowledge one of his many apt analogies— "Chartres Cathedral is like a book, its windows like its many pages."

Many thanks to my beloved teacher, the late Eva French, who introduced me Chartres Cathedral when I was her student. Miss French was also the first to show me through medieval town of Chartres, preserved within the modern town. Mr. Miller guided my further explorations through my this, my "place of the heart."

Many thanks, also, to le Centre International du Vitrail and le Musée du Vitrail, both of which are located in Chartres, France.

In this book I have woven fact and fiction to suit the overall demands of this genre, one of my favorites: Historical fiction. Here I hoped to show something of Chartres' powerful, enduring and mystical presence.

My novel was designed as an historical romance for several reasons. Many visitors to Chartres Cathedral fall in love with it and feel drawn to return, as I have, many times. The interaction of human and Divine love is part of Chartres' magic.

The most important reason, however, is the medieval world's well-known and abiding focus on romantic love. That motif seems to me the most appropriate frame and coloration for this book.

What we see of Chartres now, of course, is the finished product. Few changes have been made to the existing cathedral during its 820 years. Only indirectly, if at all, do we experience its conception, preparations, and beginnings.

Inevitably, we miss behind-the-scenes conversations, conflicts and crises omitted from official chronicles and histories.

Chartres has always prized its extraordinary and reverenced cathedral. An example of this devotion is the effort made during each World War to protect the sanctuary's priceless stained glass. Each pane of every window was carefully removed and stored until the wars' ends. Then the windows were restored to their places in the cathedral, where they remain today.

In August 1944, the American Colonel Welborn Barton Griffith, Jr., saved Chartres Cathedral during World War II. He challenged the Allied Force's plan to destroy the cathedral because the Allies suspected the Germans were occupying it. Colonel Griffith personally investigated the cathedral and found it clear of the enemy.

Because of this brave act, the destruction orders were rescinded. Colonel Griffith was killed in action soon after at Léves, a town near Chartres. The President of the United States posthumously awarded Colonel Griffith the Distinguished Service Cross and the French government awarded him the Croix de Guerre.

These are facts. However, in this novel, fiction by definition, any resemblance to persons living or dead is coincidental. ∎

Marcy Heidish,
May 5, 2014

ACKNOWLEDGMENTS

Of the many sources used for this novel, I gratefully acknowledge the most prominent:

- On-site research and numerous interviews with Malcolm Miller, author, scholar, lecturer and expert on Chartres Cathedral.
- *Blue: The Origin Of A Color,* by Michael Pasteureau.
- *Boulangerie: The Craft And Culture of Breadmaking In France,* by Paul Rambali.
- *Bread, Wine And Money: The Windows Of The Trades At Chartres Cathedral,* by Jane Welch Williams.
- *Cathedral,* by David Macauley.
- *Chartres: And The Origins Of The Cathedral,* by Titus Burckhardt.
- *Chartres Cathedral,* by Malcolm Miller.
- *Chartres: Sacred Geometry, Sacred Space,* by Gordan Strachan.

- *Chartres: The Cathdral And The Old Town*, by Malcolm Miller.
- *Daily Life In The Middle Ages*, by Paul B. Newman.
- *Glass-Painters*, by Sarah Brown and David O'Connor.
- *Heaven in Stone and Glass*, by Robert Brown.
- *Life In A Medieval City*, by Joseph and Frances Gies.
- *Life in Medieval Times*, by Marjorie Rawling.
- *Masons and Sculptors*, by Nicola Goldstream.
- *Mont-Saint-Michel and Chartres*, by Henry Adams.
- *On Divers Arts*, by Theophilus (a monk's medieval text on the process of making stained glass).
- *Stained Glass*, by Halliday and Lushington.
- *Stained Glass: Its Origins To The Present*, by Virgiia Ragnow.
- *The Art Bulletin*, volume 45, #4: "The Chronology of the Stained Glass in Chartres Cathedral," by Paul Frankl.
- *The Art Bulletin*, volume 48, #2: "On the Blues in Chartres," by Robert Sowers.
- *The Cathedral Builders*, by Jean Gimpel.
- *The Master Masons of Chartres Cathedral*, by John James.
- *The Medieval Baker's Daughter*, by Madeleine Pelner Cosman.
- *The Mysteries of Chartres Cathedral*, by Louis Charpentier. ∎

A WOMAN CALLED MOSES

*Award-winning, best-selling novel based on the life of Harriet Tubman, abolitionist and conductor on the Underground Railroad.
*Literary Guild Alternate Selection;
*A Bantam paperback.
*TV Movie, starring Cicely Tyson, still available on DVD.
*Houghton Mifflin Co., 1ˢᵗ Pub.

Praise for *A Woman Called Moses*:

Publishers Weekly: "Her story has been told before, but never as eloquently, almost poetically, as here...achingly real...a strong narrative of a totally committed woman, one who speaks directly to our own desperate need to feel committed—and our wish that somewhere in the world there were more people like Harriet Tubman."

Washington Post Book World: "Profoundly rewarding...a daring work of the imagination."

Chicago Sun Times: "Marcy Heidish has, almost uncannily, crawled into the skin and very mind of Harriet Tubman. The dialogue sings with poetic beauty."

Houghton Mifflin Co.: "As events build toward a stunning climax, we are drawn into the spellbinding narrative of an extraordinary life, and a portion of our American past." ♦♦♦

WITNESSES

WITNESSES

A Novel By Marcy Heidish

* Award-winning novel based on the life of lay minister Anne Hutchinson, <u>America's first female advocate of religious freedom</u>.
* Citations: Society for Colonial Wars; laudatory reviews; large-print, hard-cover and paperback versions.
* Houghton Mifflin Co., 1ˢᵗPub.

<u>Praise for *Witnesses:*</u>

The New York Times Book Review: " .nothing ordinary about her creation of this remarkable woman. The novel abounds in literary grace. It employs the voices of the times as though heard this minute."

The New Yorker Magazine: "A striking novel...a compelling portrait."

The Washington Post: "Pure pleasure. Anne Hutchinson is real; thanks to *Witnesses,* she at last assumes her proper place in American history." —Jonathan Yardley, Pulitzer Prize-winning critic.

Ballantine Books: "This fearless woman, mother of fifteen, a leader in medicine and politics, comes to vivid life in these pages. A true believe in religious freedom who paid dearly for her principles in two trials for heresy. In the tradition of Arthur Miller's *The Crucible*, Witnesses is the deeply felt portrait of a woman in the paranoid climate of 17ᵗʰ century Boston." ◆◆◆

THE TORCHING—The Book Store Murders

* Acclaimed contemporary novel, in hardcover and paperback.
* Literary Guild Alternate Selection; laudatory reviews.
* Optioned for TV movie.
* Simon & Schuster, 1ˢᵗ Pub.

Praise for *The Torching*:

Washington Post Book World: "Because of Heidish's skill, we get the full force of her double-whammy in part due to the grace with which she weaves the present-day and the historical, but also because of her inventiveness at the book's close, the daring way she gets both strands of plot to unite...a stylish and intelligent novelist to boot, more than up to the dizzying, tale-spinning task that she set for herself here."

Kirkus Reviews: "Shuddery mystery-suspense with supernatural overtones."

Library Journal:"Intricately constructed. A deliciously spine-tingling, multi-layered literary mystery."

Publishers Weekly: "Subtle, gratifying psychological suspense. Penetrating characterizations... Heidish impeccably orchestrates the historical and contemporary, the supernatural and psychological."

Denver Post: "Macabre ride...Eerie...Intriguing. Frightening surprises...Enjoy."

Arizona Daily Star: "An imaginative, amazing writer...A magician with words."

New York Daily News: "Compellingly readable and likely to induce the screaming-meemies." ♦♦♦

THE SECRET ANNIE OAKLEY

* Acclaimed novel based on the life of the legendary sharp-shooter.
* Hard- and Paperback versions
* A *Readers Digest* Condensed Novel.
* Optioned for film.
*Translated into several languages, laudatory reviews.
*New American Library, 1st Pub.

Praise for *The Secret Annie Oakley:*

Kirkus Reviews: "An immensely touching and cohesive fictional biography of the legendary sharp-shooter builds from exemplary research to a fresh portrait of a talented woman in crisis, a class act —as Heidish reconstructs. with color and drama, the choreography of the shows, the tone of the period, and the textures of a haunting past."

The Arizona Daily Star: "...an imaginative, amazing writer...a magician with words. Each character has been brought to life with a mere pen stroke; flesh and blood beings that are more than fiction. A master-piece of creative writing."

The Kansas City Star: "An unforgettable story."
Christian Science Monitor: "...Marcy Heidish weaves historical facts into a novel so moving that there will be many times in the years to come that I'll take pleasure in remembering that stout-hearted woman. 'Annie Oakley' hits the bull's eye every time." ♦♦♦

MIRACLES

MIRACLES

A Novel By Marcy Heidish

* Historical novel based on the life of **Mother Elizabeth Seton**, first American-born canonized saint.

* Main selection, *The Catholic Book Club*.

*New American Library, 1st Pub.

Praise for *Miracles*:

The New York Times Book Review: "This appealing book, told from the point of view of a skeptical modern priest, moves swiftly through tragedy to triumph."

Kirkus Reviews: "Working delicately with a balance of Church hagiography and psychological insight, Ms. Heidish provides another strong focus on the root dilemma of female saints and achievers."

New American Library: "*Miracles* is the story of an unforgettable woman's life and love. It is a novel charged with the vitality of a life that saw many changes, and with the power of a love that took many forms.[whether] as a lonely daughter of a wealthy, indifferent man; a searching young woman; a contented matron embracing a marriage that produced five beloved children; a widow searching for new meaning to life." ♦♦♦

DEADLINE

* Contemporary psychological novel with a "mystery" as a narrative line.
* Nominee for prestigious national "Edgar" Award; fine reviews.
* St. Martin's Press, 1ˢᵗ Pub.

Praise for *Deadline*:

Washington Post: "*Deadline* is a tense, well-turned tale, filled with authentic police and newspaper people. Heidish's taut, punchy style moves the story at lightning speed."

Kirkus Reviews: "The high-tension plot is enhanced by sharply etched pictures, by many vivid characters, and by a crisp, clean, first-person style. Heidish imbues her haunting story and her gutsy heroine with a rare sense of tenderness and poignancy. An impressive mystery by a gifted writer."

St. Martin's Press: "This wire-tight novel probes relentlessly, driving deep into psychological darkness and violent death. As the riveting story reaches its stunning conclusion, we see a complex woman forced to meet the ultimate deadline." ◆◆◆

A Dangerous Woman: Mother Jones, An Unsung American Heroine

 *A compelling, inspiring new historical novel, another powerful "profile in courage" American-style novel based on the life of Mary Harris Jones, a self-proclaimed Hell Raiser, daring labor leader, and colorful, quirky humanitarian.

*The arresting novel of an indomitable force, dressed demurely in widow's weeds and lace collars who:

> As an Irish immigrant—lost her homeland to the Great Famine.

> As a wife and mother—lost her whole family to yellow fever.

> As a dressmaker—lost home and business to the Chicago Fire

> As a survivor—turned from sorrow to help others survive.

Follow one of America's most feisty, fearless...and forgotten heroines whose rallying cry was:

"PRAY FOR THE DEAD—AND FIGHT LIKE HELL FOR THE LIVING!" ♦♦♦

DESTINED TO DANCE: A Novel About Martha Graham

> They called her a genius.
> They called her a goddess.
> They called her a monster.

Which title best fits Martha Graham, iconic Mother of Modern Dance? Find out—in the <u>first historical novel about this great American diva</u>.

DESTINED TO DANCE is a creative portrait of the legendary dancer and choreographer. Heidish offers another remarkable account of an American heroine: her successes, her sorrows, and her struggles.

Here is a masterful portrait of Graham, on stage, backstage, offstage. We see Graham's breakthrough brilliance, often compared to Picasso's or Stravinsky.

We also witness Graham's triumph over alcoholism, despair, and a failed marriage. Set against the intriguing world of dance, Martha Graham's story offers us a close-up on a complex and compelling overcomer.

Martha Graham (1894-1991) invented a new "language of movement," still taught around the world and exemplified in such classic works as *Appalachian Spring*, among 180 others.

As always, Heidish's research is thorough and her sense of her subject is magical. For all who love the arts, all who seek inspiration, and all who like to read between history's lines, *DESTINED TO DANCE* is a must-read book.   ♦♦♦

NON-FICTION BOOKS:
Soul and the City
WaterBrook Press, Random House imprint

Praise for *Soul and the City*:

*"I actually started reading Marcy Heidish's *Soul and the City* on a subway train. I must say it had exactly the effect she writes about: it gave me peace in the middle of the hurry, the rush, the loud noise of the city."

—Rick Hamlin, executive editor, Guideposts; author of *Finding God on the A Train*

* "Marcy Heidish has compiled a rich and nuanced touring companion to rival any Michelin or Eye-witness guide—usable in any city of the world. Keep it close and you will meet beauty and holiness no matter where you pause to look."

— Leigh McLeroy, author of *The Beautiful Ache* and *The Sacred Ordinary*

* "*Soul and the City* is a deeply inspiring call to awareness to connection with God and with others, and ultimately to soulful worship through so many aspects of life in the city that we find mundane, undesirable, or that even go unnoticed. Almost instantly, upon delving into its pages, you find your perspective changed."

— Sarah Zacharias Davis, author of *Confessions from an Honest Wife, Transparent, and The Friends We Keep.* ♦♦♦

Defiant Daughters
Liguori Publications.

Praise for *Defiant Daughters*:

What do
Joan of Arc,
Immaculée Ilibagiza,
Corrie ten Boom, and
Sojourner Truth
have in common?

These women are among those whom best-selling author Marcy Heidish calls "Defiant Daughters."

This informative, challenging, and entertaining book spotlights the lives of more than 20 spiritual trail-blazers and their responses to crises of conscience.

They represent different races, denominations, and nations, but all are feisty—often fiery—and always faithful to their callings.

Heidish seeks out the decisive juncture where each took a stand for conscience, however high the cost.

This stunning and compelling book will bring you face-to-face with an unforgettable female gallery of "profiles in courage."

— Liguori Publications ♦♦♦

A Candle At Midnight
Ave Maria Press

A Candle At Midnight

By Marcy Heidish

Praise for *A Candle At Midnight*:

* "Heidish honors modern medicine and spiritual healing in this compelling work."
— Alen J. Salerian, M.D., Medical Director of the Washington Psychiatric Center

* "This is not a book of abstractions. I recommend this book to anyone who is caught in the darkness of mid-night."
— Martha Manning, Author of *Undercurrents: A Life Beneath the Surface*:

* "A masterpiece!"
— Rev. Nancy Eggert, Spiritual Director ♦♦♦

Who Cares? Simple Ways YOU Can Reach Out
Ave Maria Press

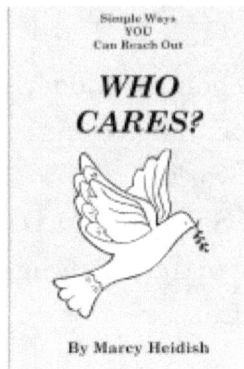

Praise for *Who Cares?*:

A lonely neighbor, a colleague in distress, a friend in difficulty. In situations like these we want to reach out and help, yet so often we feel unsure about our response.

What to do?
What to say?
What is enough?
Too much?
Too little?

This practical book is designed to bring out the caring person in each of us. Marcy Heidish offers simple, specific ways to practice the art of caring, especially within our immediate circle of concern: family, friends, neighbors, and coworkers.

Heidish reminds us of the many little things we can do to open the door to a caring relationship.
— Ave Maria Press

"Contains savvy insights and wisdom about service. This is an ideal resource for anyone interested in engaged spirituality."
— *Cultural Information Service*: ♦♦♦

Too Late To Be A Fortune Cookie Writer

"A novelist has a specific poetic license which also applies to his own life."
~ Jerzi Kosinski

Marcy Heidish, award-winning author of fourteen books, fiction and non-fiction, is just such a novelist with a "specific poetic license."

Her work has been praised for its "lyrical grace" and so it is a special joy to present her first book of poetry. Ms. Heidish has written poems for decades.

With humor and humanity, this collection spans a broad range of subjects. Insight, wit and depth enliven these poems. They address universal concerns: maturity, mortality, memory and much more.

Ms. Heidish gives us an intimate glimpse into a writer's soul. Adept at varied verse forms, she amuses, reflects, recalls, and rejoices:

• "A watched pot never boils unless you're boiling vodka."

• "Houses crowd my life like chairs on a November beach."

• "The sun is a peach, half ripened, at hand."

And the poet brings us with her. ◆◆◆

Short Pieces:

Articles and book reviews published in *Ms.* Magazine, *GEO* Magazine, *The Washington Post*, *The Washington Star*, and various in-flight periodicals.

Two of these pieces are:

> ** The Pilgrim Who Stayed*, *GEO* Magazine, about Chartres Cathedral, widely translated.

> ** The Grand Dame of the Harbor*, about the Statue of Liberty, was a highly acclaimed cover story for *GEO* Magazine. This article is included in a textbook anthology designed to teach writing to college students. Winner of coveted Apex Award. ◆◆◆

See Marcy Heidish page at:
www.Amazon.com
[AND Kindle] *

* Marcy Heidish Books are printed by Lightning Source and distributed by Ingram of Ingram Content Group Inc., the world's largest distributor of physical and digital content, providing books, music and media content to over 38,000 retailers, libraries, schools and distribution partners in 195 countries. More than 25,000 publishers use Ingram's . ◆◆◆